Washtenaw Library for the
Blind & Physically Disabled
@ AADL

Ha
ou
for
hir
pay
an
int
wo
the
be
for
rev

If you are only able to read large print, you may qualify for WLBPD @ AADL services, including receiving audio and large print books by mail at no charge.

For more information:

Email • wlbpd@aadl.org
Phone • (734) 327-4224
Website • wlbpd.aadl.org

This for S. and N.,
when the time comes

GO HANG
THE MAN

by
Dan Claymaker

Dales Large Print Books
Long Preston, North Yorkshire,
England.

British Library Cataloguing in Publication Data.

Claymaker, Dan
    Go hang the man.

A catalogue record for this book is
available from the British Library

ISBN 1-85389-945-3 pbk

First published in Great Britain by Robert Hale Ltd., 1998

Copyright © 1998 by Dan Claymaker

Cover illustration © Lopez by arrangement with Norma
Editorial S.A

Dales Large Print is an imprint of
Library Magna Books Ltd.
Printed and bound in Great Britain by
T.J. International Ltd., Cornwall, PL28 8RW.

ONE

He was out—free as a high hawk, mean-eyed hungry, and riding hard for Benefice. That was how the folk there got to hear that Frank Quinton had served his five-year sentence in the Pen at Jamesville and was coming back. That was the news brought in on the regular stage that set them to figuring it would take him maybe seven days to reach them and less than an hour to vent his hatred and settle old scores. And it was that, the thought of Quinton on the rampage, that decided them to stop him any way they could before he reached town—*if* they could.

But that was not how it began all those years ago ...

Summer came early that year, hot and

thick and sticky, tight as an old breath over the remote plains' town of Benefice where by mid-July Sheriff Legget Rand was already counting down the hours to boiling point.

Heat and flies and stifling days that ushered in long airless nights got to folk like a tireless itch, he reckoned. No matter how much or how regular a man scratched, the irritation stayed until it seemed he was just heat spooked and might go mad. Too little to do and no incentive to do it, too many days spent lazing—and a darned sight too much to drink—set to making fellows quarrelsome, worked through their minds like termites boring out the holes where petty disputes bred and fed and grew to fighting issues.

He could see it everywhere that summer: in the normally quiet homes, where normally quiet men beat their normally quiet wives for no better reason than that nothing and nobody was normal and everything too quiet that year; in the street, where one-time busy folk busied themselves with nothing more important than seeking out the shade and coming close to brawling when the choice cooler spots were taken; in the livery, where horses fretted in confining sweat and Jake Mullen gave up shoeing and beating out hot iron over heat he could not face; in the store, where folk came to bartering prices; in the barber's shop, where men lathered up twice daily for the touch of water and complained when Charlie Piecemeal rationed it; in the outskirt homesteads, where hogs had no place to wallow and got kicked for their grunting; and most of all in Hooper's Saloon.

There was trouble there all day, every day, and most nights, too, for those with the wherewithal to be there. Nothing in the early days that Sheriff Rand could not handle with a few choice curses and the threat of a drawn Colt, but it was getting worse and Willard Hooper and his collection of frowzy ceiling experts in their worn-out dresses was no help. He simply cashed in on insatiable thirsts and farmed out the girls half-price to those still standing. One of these nights there would be real trouble, of the blood-spilling kind.

And then Quinton rode in.

Came through the dusty haze soon after sun-up one heat-soaked morning. No reason for him being there that Rand could see or fathom from the quiet-spoken, dark-eyed stranger. He just arrived, hitched his mount back of the livery and took a room at Hooper's. Stayed there for the most part, too, save to eat, drink two fingers of tonsil paint, and always alone, never any company sought or encouraged. A real loner, silent as the grave. But there was something about him even then that bothered Rand.

Maybe it was the fellow's silence, or maybe it was the way he watched, like he was a hawk waiting for the right prey to pass his way. Could be those twin Colts he always wore; shiny, well-handled butts staring out of polished leather holsters. Or was it that Quinton seemed to be the only man in town not troubled by the heat? Fellow never broke sweat, not even in the blaze of noon; never walked in the shade or opened the window of his room. Never, come to that, did much at all. And that pestered Rand worse than the flies.

Not that he had the time to give Frank Quinton a deal of thought on the night the whole heat-bubbling pot that was Benefice finally boiled over.

Trouble started, sure enough, at Hooper's. Things had been fairly quiet there for most of the night—the usual tipping out of stone-eyed drunks, the familiar forays into grabbing half-asleep bar girls, Willard Hooper's gaze glinting dollar bills—but all that had changed over a game of poker.

Sam Betts had accused Ben Little of cheating doubtless rightly so bearing in mind Ben's paranoid aversion to losing—and jumped to his feet in a lather of anger and foul-mouthed curses, one hand fumbling for the butt of his ancient .45. Matter in normal circumstances might have ended there with Sam finally backing off under the restraining hand of somebody offering to buy him a beer, but these circumstances were far from normal.

There had been no restraining hand, no offer of a beer, only a long, sweaty silence in which nobody moved, nobody spoke or so much as belched. Sam's fingers got itchy; Ben Little simply blinked his slow way to his feet and without another word shot Sam clean through the chest from a draw that cleared leather faster than a fellow could swallow.

And that, a single shot released in the haze of heat and stifling smoke-filled air, had been the touch-light to the mayhem that followed.

Three men grabbed Ben and disarmed him. The bar girls started screaming. Hooper yelled, but nobody heard or took the slightest notice. A fight began far side of the room, another in a darkened corner. Tables and chairs were thrown aside, glasses and bottles crashed to gleaming shards, windows smashed, a batwing torn from its hinges. Two men threw a third to the back of the bar; a red-haired girl had her dress ripped from her sweating body and ran screeching for the stairs to the upstairs rooms, but never made it under the lunge of a body that smothered her. Men flung fists, kicked and cursed at anything that moved, shadows included, and within minutes had reduced Hooper's bar to a ramshackle heap, a blood-soaked, sweat-smeared wreck.

Seconds later, when there was nothing left to smash and the men stood dripping, near-exhausted, a lone voice from somewhere deep in the chaos croaked the few clipped phrases that were to seal the fate of Benefice in shame.

'Ben Little'll hang for this! Hang by his goddamn neck! Let's go hang the man—right now!'

TWO

Sheriff Legget Rand met the mob head-on as they tumbled from the saloon to the street. No need for a second, closer look, to measure the men's intent or figure where they were heading. It was all plain enough: in the crazed glow in their eyes, the sweat-lathered faces, heaving chests, anxious hands, growls and hissing curses—and not least in the sight of that rope already tight at Ben Little's neck.

'Hold on there,' yelled Rand, halting the mob with a menacing sweep of his Winchester. 'Just what in hell's name—'

'Don't interfere none, Sheriff,' came a dusty, croaking voice from the crowd. 'This sonofabitch is for hangin'. Hangin', we say, and hang he will! So step aside while we get to it.'

13

'Not in my town,' snapped Rand. 'That's a lynchin' yuh plannin' there.'

'Shot Sam Betts clean through he did,' came another voice. 'Poor devil never stood a chance.'

'Cheatin' scumbag!'

'Hound dung!'

'Not fit to stay breathin'!'

'Hang the dog!'

'Yeah, hang him! See the bastard kickin'!'

'Hang him! Hang him!'

The chant rose on the thick night air until the sound of it bounced from every building, echoed round every steaming corner and filled Rand's ears like a piercing scream. He yelled another warning to stand back, swung the Winchester through another threatening arc, but the men were moving again, slowly now, silently, their faces wet with hatred, a gleaming madness that burned at their flesh as if the very flame of that summer had set them alight.

Rand began to back, the rifle tight in

his grip, sweat soaking through his shirt. He saw the petrified glaze in Ben Little's eyes as he stumbled like a tethered steer at the end of the rope, his limbs already twitching in anticipation of the agony to come. Goddamnit, there was no way this mob were going to be held, he thought, swinging the rifle again, not without letting the Winchester rip into them; not without a half-dozen heat-crazed men spilling their blood in a moment of madness.

Could he do that? Would he?

Rand raised the rifle a fraction and fired two fast shots high above the men's heads. 'That's just a warning,' he called as the echo whined and died. 'Next time is for real.'

'Back off, Legget,' snarled a man in the front line. 'This is town business.'

'Fool's fever,' mouthed Rand, stiffening the rifle ahead of him, but easing back a step as the mob began to move again. He glanced quickly to the left, to the huddle of women in the darkness of the boardwalk, Doe Raynes shuffling among them like a demented nursemaid, consoling, protecting, not knowing who to turn to next. To the right and the still, dark shape of that fellow Quinton, standing there, just watching, waiting. Why the hell not make a move, wondered Rand, step down to the street and lend a hand? Why just stand there like a one-man audience witnessing a town tear itself apart, bury itself? Why not ...

Rand never knew who fired the shots or truly where they came from, only that the first buried itself deep in his thigh, the second skimming like a white-hot coal across his temple as he lost his grip on the Winchester, heard it thud to the ground, and then followed it, the mob pouring over his sprawled body in a baying, sweating mass, intent at any price on reaching all they could see—the hanging tree far end of the street.

They hanged Ben Little on the stroke

of midnight and left his body dangling there, end of a taut, creaking rope, until sun-up. And when that was done the folk of Benefice went back to sweating out their heatwave summer without much talk, save in hushed whispers, of what had happened, but with the haunting of it settled in their silent thoughts and their public conscience eased some when they gratefully, willingly pointed the finger of Judas at Frank Quinton as the man whose hand had been on the noose that dreadful night.

How it was, or by what chance, it came to be that Marshal John Edgeworth rode into town at dawn that morning, saw the hanged man still there on the tree and wanted to know how come, no one ever bothered to ask. They were only too relieved to have Quinton still there at Hooper's, a stranger, not one of them, somebody they could easily blame and afford to lose without a qualm. After all, who knew him or why he was here? Just a drifter. Disposable. Who cared, anyhow? Folk would soon forget.

'Yuh reckon?' Doc Raynes had croaked eerily.

Sheriff Legget Rand knew nothing of this until the morning, two days later, he regained full consciousness to find himself in bed in a back room at Hooper's, his head and leg in bandages, a bottle of cheap whiskey at his side, his clothes draped neatly over a chair facing him.

First thing he noticed was that his badge was missing from his waistcoat. Second thing was the man standing by the window watching a drift of light rain spit across it.

'Yuh made it,' said the man, leaning back against the wall, folding his arms across the tailored cut of his frock coat, twitching a corner of his smoke-stained moustache. 'Howdy. Name's Edgeworth— Marshal John Edgeworth. Pleased to meet yuh, Mister Rand. How yuh feelin'?' The marshal's blue eyes twinkled through his ready smile. 'Stupid question. Forget it. I can see for m'self.'

Rand eased himself higher on the pillows, blinked and wiped a hand across his face. 'What's with the mister?' he asked. 'I'm sheriff here, *Mister* Edgeworth.'

'Well, yuh were 'til a day ago. Seems like the town folk don't reckon yuh'll be up to it no more.'

Rand blinked again. 'What the hell yuh talkin' about, and just what yuh doin' on my patch, anyhow?'

'Hold on there, Rand. Take it easy. Ain't no point in pushin' that fever higher than it already is.' The marshal unfolded his arms, slid his hands to his pockets and crossed to the foot of the bed. 'Yuh got a minute or so there and I'll explain.'

'Yuh'd just better,' croaked Rand, 'otherwise—'

'Fact is,' said Edgeworth in a barbed, sharper tone, 'yuh had some real trouble here, and that's puttin' it mildly. Lucky I happened by.'

19

Rand struggled higher on the pillows. 'Look here, mister—Marshal—whatever yuh damned well are—'

'I been sittin' on Frank Quinton's tail for a coupla months,' Edgeworth went on dismissively. 'Wanted back Salton way on suspicion of ridin' with the Whittaker gang. Rape, robbery—the usual score. No real hard evidence against the fella, but now I got him for his part in a murder don't matter much, anyhow.'

'Quinton? Murder?' coughed Rand. 'That's about as mule-headed crazy as—'

'Well, yuh'd hardly know now, would yuh,' snapped the marshal, 'seein' as yuh were out cold there in the street time of the hangin'.'

'Yuh mean they did it—hanged Ben Little?' groaned Rand, beginning to sweat. 'Lynched him?'

Edgeworth dug his hands deeper into his pockets. 'Not quite the way I hear it,' he went on coolly. 'Quinton did the hangin'. It was his hand there on the noose, his hand that cleared the horse from under Little. Don't seem to be no question of it. Plenty enough witnesses.'

'Yuh bet yuh sweet life there were witnesses—the whole damned town! That was a lynchin', mister, plain as the nose on yuh face.'

'Well, there may have been others involved,' shrugged Edgeworth, 'but I ain't fussed none one way or the other. I got Quinton and all the sworn statements I need to put him away in Jamesville for a minimum of five. Makes them two months trailin' him seem worthwhile.'

Rand groaned again and came still higher on the pillows. 'Yuh got this all wrong, Marshal,' he spluttered. 'Wrong as yuh can get. I'll tell yuh what happened and put names to those who did it. As for Quinton ... Now you listen good, mister, real good while I get this straight.'

'No, fella, you listen good,' said Edgeworth, stiffening, ' 'cus I'm kinda in a hurry to clear this town and get my prisoner back to Salton, so I'll say what I have to just once, then take my leave. I don't know the detail of what went on in this town two nights back and, frankly, I ain't askin'. That's for the folk here to sort out best they can. Like I say, I got my man. Quinton's goin' to jail for his part in the hangin' of Ben Little and there's no shortage of proof. That's good enough for me.'

'But it just ain't so,' spluttered Rand. 'I was there f'Crissake! Out there, tryin' to hold that heat-crazed mob back from what they planned. I saw Quinton and he weren't even a part of it—I swear on my badge he weren't.'

'Yeah, oh, and that's another thing,' said Edgeworth, lowering his gaze for a moment. 'That badge—it ain't yours no more as I understand it. Doc reckons that wound there in yuh leg'll leave yuh with a permanent limp, and Benefice don't seem one bit keen on havin' a limpin' sheriff. Rough, but that's the way of it.

22

Yuh town elders have handed the badge to Luce Whitworth. Unanimous decision. Sorry. Don't take it too hard on yourself. Hazard of the job, I guess.'

Rand groaned deep in his throat and lay back on the pillows. 'Sonofabitch,' he croaked, and closed his eyes.

When he opened them again the room was empty, silent save for the steady beat of rain at the window, the sound of his own deep, troubled breathing. He blinked against the gloom and thought that just for a second he saw a shape moving across the room. The shape of a man, tall and dark as the night.

The haunting had begun.

chew over the
:, like they were
led bone. Willard
narlie Piecemeal,
orth, them and a
mories were long
this night as they
e the lynching of
Ben Little.

Only this time there was something different, thought Legget Rand, watching them from his usual table in a corner of Hooper's Saloon. Very different. This night their fear was real, etched in grey lines on their faces, in the shifty glaze to their eyes, the darting glances, twitchy fingers. Real and alive and beginning to gnaw.

He eased back in his chair, rubbed a

hand over his aching leg, and watched Willard Hooper pace the few yards to the bar, turn and lean back on it.

'Well,' he asked, gazing over the assembled faces, 'we just goin' to sit here talkin', or are we goin' to get to doin'? Time's runnin' out. We got five days at most, mebbe less if Quinton's ridin' hard, and yuh can bet he's doin' just that.'

'I say we sit tight,' came a voice from a cloud of smoke. 'Let Quinton come to us. We can handle him.'

'Yuh figure so?' said Charlie Piecemeal. 'Just like that, eh? Stand out there and gun him down? That easy?'

'Hell, it's been five years,' said Jake Mullen, wiping beer froth from his stubble. 'No tellin' what sorta shape the fella's in. Jamesville ain't no picnic. Nossir. I heard say as how—'

'He'll be all worn through,' came another voice. 'A wreck. No fit state to go pickin' fights, not no how. I seen fellas out of Jamesville, and they ain't a pretty sight.

Most can't hardly stand, let alone fight.'

'This fella will,' said Doc Raynes quietly. 'Oh, yes, this fella will. He's had five long years to plan on ridin' back to Benefice. Five years to wait and keep himself ready. He'll fight, sure enough, just like he's been fightin' to stay alive in Jamesville.'

'So what yuh sayin', Doc?' asked Hooper.

Doc Raynes was thoughtful for a moment, his fingers tapping lightly on the table. 'Yuh got two choices,' he began again. 'Yuh could ride out, a half-dozen or so of yuh, try to stop him before he gets close. If yuh don't he'll rip this town apart single-handed. Sure, he'll die eventually, but there'll be a bloodbath here the likes of which yuh never seen. Or—'

'Yeah, or what?' echoed a voice.

'We could come clean, all of us, go tell Marshal Edgeworth at Salton what really happened here that night, see if we could win a pardon for Quinton.'

There was a deep, heavy silence for what

seemed minutes until a chair was pushed back by a man with a round, sweating face and whiskey-bright eyes. 'Say that again, Doc,' he croaked, coming unsteadily to his feet.

'Yuh heard,' said Raynes. 'Them's yuh choices. Ain't no others open to us.'

'Hell!' snapped Charlie Piecemeal. 'Them ain't choices. Them's suicide! Specially the last one. I ain't puttin' my life on the line in some two-bit jail for nobody. I say we get to Quinton first. Get it over with. Shoot the fella before he gets a sniff of town. We could do it. Six guns against one. 'Course we could.'

There were murmurs, then shouts of agreement.

'Luce, what yuh say?' asked Hooper. 'Yuh reckon we could?'

Legget Rand shifted impatiently as the young sheriff sauntered to the centre of the room. 'Sure,' said Whitworth through a soft, sly grin. 'No reason why not. Plan it careful, go easy. Quinton won't be expectin' no reception, that's for certain. We got surprise on our side. We got the edge. That's what counts.' His fingers slid like snakes over the butt of his holstered Colt. 'Yeah, we could do it.'

Doc Raynes opened his mouth but stayed silent. Luce Whitworth glowed in the slaps of approval across his shoulders. Willard Hooper glanced quickly at Rand, then thudded a fist on the bar.

'OK, OK,' he called. 'So it seems we're agreed. We stop Quinton before he gets to town. Now, who's volunteerin' to ride? Who's willin' to go out there and kill the sonofabitch?'

Legget Rand sat long into that night in the room above the general store he had made his home, and pondered the chances of pulling off the crazy notion that had entered his head at the close of the meeting in Hooper's.

Was it a hopeless long shot? Had his thinking gone plumb wild, was he spooked out of his mind, scrambling blind in a brainstorm, or had he finally come to his senses and was seeing things clear for the first time in years?

Damn it, that plan of Hooper's to ride out and face Quinton before he hit town was no less crazy, especially with an itchy gun like Luce Whitworth heading it up. Did any one of those who would ride with him seriously believe that Quinton could be stopped as easy as simply crossing his trail and gunning him down? Had nobody reckoned on the fellow's state of mind? Had they forgotten that Quinton had served five long years in a personal hell; five years of living in a hole with his seething anger, the burning hatred, and then all the time in the world to plan just how and when he would seek his revenge, settle the scores for that night of the lynching?

When Frank Quinton had squinted his first sight of real light on the day of his release he had been looking only one way—clear-eyed to Benefice. And he had already lived out a thousand times how he would get there. There was not a man on this earth who could stop him.

Trouble was, pondered Rand, the whole town was gripped in a fever of conscience. The ghost of their past had risen, save that this ghost was no grey-mist apparition set on just haunting. This ghost was real, alive, flesh and blood, with real guns and a reason to use them. And folk knew it. They were in for as big a sweat now as they had ever lathered up five years ago.

But maybe there was a way to avoid what Doc Raynes had reckoned would be a bloodbath. There was no man with courage enough to go tell Edgeworth the truth; no, damn it, they would sooner wallow in more death, watch Benefice sink deeper into the Devil's cauldron it had brewed for itself, but there was a man prepared to go find Quinton and try reasoning with him before

Marshal Edgeworth had a genuine reason for locking him back in Jamesville—or watching him hang.

That man, too, had paid a high price for being in Benefice that night; lost his job, been part crippled, left to live on whatever dregs Willard Hooper slopped his way, reduced to sitting alone most nights with only his thoughts. He had served a sentence of a kind. Maybe the time had come for his release.

Maybe his notion was not so crazy after all.

Six men saddled up and reined their mounts north on the trail for Jamesville at sun-up the following morning: Luce Whitworth, Willard Hooper, Charlie Piecemeal, Jake Mullen, and two of Whitworth's deputies, names of Bob Sharman and Vince Claim. They were fitted out for five days' riding and living rough and were seen off by just about the whole population of Benefice who had not slept easy that night and had waited impatiently for the dawn.

Legget Rand had left town silently and unseen two hours ahead of them.

FOUR

Quinton staggered to the top of the ridge, spat the dirt and dust from his parched mouth and fell exhausted, sweat-soaked and gasping into the burning sand. He lay there a full minute before rolling over, heaving himself into a sitting position and pulling off his boots.

He sighed with relief, then winced at the sight of the blistered, broken skin across his toes and heels. Hell, he would give a lot right now for a pair of socks and boots that boasted real soles and something better than paper-thin leather, maybe more than he would give for a pan of cool water. Not, he reflected, that he had so much as half a bean to give for either. He spat and sighed again and came slowly to his feet. So what awaited far side of this goddamn ridge?

Not a deal, he thought, as his eyes squinted against the unrelenting glare. More sand, more rocks, more outcrops, gulches, draws and dirt—more of every sonofabitch torment he had already faced. He fixed his hands on his hips and swung his gaze from left to right. No hint of the trail. Must run deeper south. No tracks either. Only wilderness. Well, just how far could a fellow walk barefoot through that sort of hell? Couple of miles? Three if he got lucky? Three miles to nowhere!

Turnkey back there at Jamesville had been right. 'On yuh way, Quinton,' he had grinned sardonically, letting his prisoner loose on the desert. 'Not that yuh'll get far. Most never do. No horse, no sidearms, just yuh hat and what yuh stand in. Give yuh a couple days. No more.' The man's great belly had rolled in his laughter. 'And we don't collect dead bodies neither. Leave 'em for the crows! See yuh, Quinton—though I doubt it!'

Sonofabitch! But maybe the fellow had

been closer to the truth. This was no place for a man without a horse, and without a horse a man would soon be no man at all, just crow-meat, specially if he got to dwelling on it.

Quinton grunted to himself. There would be no dwelling on anything save what had been in his mind these five long years: Benefice and getting there. Just that, and putting a whole heap of wrongs fiercely right. He grunted again. So how to see those five years satisfied, he pondered: stagger on; trust to the Good Lord; get lucky? 'No choice, Quinton,' he croaked, 'none at all ...' And turned to collect his so-called boots.

It was that, the half turn, the lowering of his line of vision, that set his heart beating.

Smoke! That was definitely smoke out there. Mile to the west. A slow, spiralling curl of grey. First smoke from a freshly lit fire below a dip of the land. Wagon-train, drifters? Who cared? Smoke meant folk out here, and folk of any kind were all he needed right now.

He picked up his boots and staggered on.

But it was to be another whole hour of sun-baked agony before Quinton came within reach of the source of the smoke and, by then, his already hazy vision was almost too blurred to identify it.

No drawn-up wagons, that was for sure, and no drifters either. No, this was a deal more—a homestead of sorts, as best he could make out; nothing grand or prosperous; in sore need of repair, specially the roof, but somebody was scratching a living out of the surrounding scorched dirt. Or waiting for death.

Quinton squatted among the rocks watching the place, some other sign of life, for another half-hour. He was in desperate need of water now, fretting, too, over the gnawing ache in his belly for food, but if five years in Jamesville had taught him anything it was that nothing, but nothing, was ever quite what it seemed. Sometimes paid a fellow to sit tight and wait. A thirsty man could rush for water and never make it to the trough, or worse, find it bone-dry and empty. So hold your reins, Quinton, he mused, and stay watching.

The movement came suddenly, a purposeful opening of the door and the appearance in the slim shade cast from the roof of a woman, tousle-haired, tired and dirt-stained, bedraggled in a worn, patched dress that had long since seen better days. She was carrying a wooden pail, moving to the back of the building now to a water-butt. Drinking water only, thought Quinton, judging by the state of the woman.

He squatted where he was, still watching the open door, wondering if the woman might be followed by her man, but the space stayed empty and nothing moved until she reappeared straining under the weight of the brimming pail of water.

She slopped some to a puddle that sizzled and was a dark stain instantly in the dirt. Quinton groaned and licked his dry, cracked lips as the woman struggled indoors again and slammed the door shut.

Hell, now what, he wondered? Go down there, stagger to the door and simply wait for the woman to open it? Her, or whoever lived there with her? There had to be somebody, surely? Or was he reading this all wrong. Maybe her man was out some place. No sign of any mounts around, no wagon, buckboard, nothing save the tumbledown home and that water-butt out back.

Water ... It was the thought of it, the lure of it, that decided Quinton in that next moment. He needed water, had to have it, if he was to see this day through—and that he was going to do whatever the price.

He came slowly to his feet, stiff now with the ache of exhaustion, soaked with salty sweat, forced to measure each step, will himself into making it. But his gaze stayed tight on the homestead door and the window to the side of it. Not, he figured, that he was in any condition to do anything about a movement at either. If somebody had a Winchester trained on him right now ...

Somebody had.

He saw the glint of the barrel as the window eased open a fraction, watched it level, steady on its target. He was plumb in line with no place to go, no cover to dive for even if he could summon the strength, and nothing to answer with save his voice, always assuming he could raise that above a croak. No, if whoever was at the end of that barrel had a mind to fire he could have a dead body any time he chose.

Quinton came on at the same pace, stifling his winces as his bare, blistered feet scraped over the dirt, every pebble burning into the flesh like a flaming coal. His arms hung loose at his sides, but he strained with every fibre in him to hold his head high, keep his gaze steady, watch the probing gleam of that barrel. He would see the blaze of the shot for an instant when it came, feel the heat of the lead burn through him. Then there would be nothing. Five years' planning would end right here in a nowhere place, shot at the whim of a nobody he never got to seeing properly.

Four more steps, five, six ... Goddamnit, how close did he have to get before that trigger-finger lost its patience? He was almost there now, no more than a few agonizing steps from the shade. Maybe he could make a rush for the back, get to the water. No chance. No strength for anything like a rush to anywhere. So maybe he should ease up, halt where he was. Hell, anybody could see clear enough he was not armed.

He stopped, swayed, blinked, licked at his lips. Give it ten seconds and he would pass out, never hear the shot, maybe never feel it. His blurred heat-shimmered gaze slid to the window. Where was the barrel, damn it, where had it shifted? Was he going to take the ripping blaze from the door? Would it be flung open just before he collapsed? What would he see first, the barrel or the killer behind it? What would he see last?

All Quinton did see when the door opened was a wave of water, white as a low scudding cloud, heading his way from the pail. And all he felt before he passed out was the cool, clear, life-giving blast of it full in his face.

FIVE

He was back with the shadows, lurking, tightening, until it seemed they would suffocate. Prison shadows. Jamesville shadows.

But this was no prison, no way. This was some place else, somewhere Quinton had never been, save that he could feel it in his still damp, clinging shirt and pants, in the easy, sundown cool on his face. This was where he had staggered from the desert—the tumbledown homestead with its curl of smoke, the woman, the gleaming Winchester barrel, and then ...

Quinton waited another minute before opening his eyes fully on the room. The shadows, friendlier now, were thrown from the soft glow of a lantern set somewhere to the right of the bed where he lay. His gaze traced the beamed ceiling pitted with empty hooks swathed in a network of cobwebs. He watched a spider scurry for cover, then eased his head slowly to the left. An old dresser with cracked, broken drawers; a jug, bowl, hairbrush with half the bristles missing, plate, skinning knife, and sand—sand covering everything like it was breeding where it lay.

He swallowed, waited again, listening but hearing nothing, then turned his head to the right, to the glow of light.

The woman was seated at the side of the lantern, her stare from her tired blue eyes fixed firmly on him. She was still tousle-haired, bedraggled, dirt-stained, but with her hands firm on the rifle cradled across her lap. Quinton watched her fingers flicker over the trigger, and raised a wan smile with his grunt.

'Howdy,' he murmured.

The woman brushed loose strands of corn-coloured hair from her cheek. 'Yuh needed that,' she said quietly. 'The water and the sleep. Yuh feelin' better?'

'Much,' said Quinton, raising himself on one elbow. 'Thanks. Yuh saved what was left of me out there.'

The woman's fingers relaxed. 'Took yuh for some no-good drifter first off. Might have blown yuh clean apart, 'til I saw yuh boots. Yuh been walkin' some. Outa Jamesville?'

'Released a day or so back, just as yuh see me.'

'Figured so. Seen 'em before from time to time.' The woman slid the rifle to the floor. 'Lucky yuh headed this way. Most don't. They just die.' Her eyes narrowed. 'Why this way, mister? Any particular reason?'

'Headin' for Benefice, ma'am,' said Quinton, easing his legs clear of the bed to sit upright.

'Benefice, f'Crissake,' frowned the woman. 'Hell that's some walk. Yuh'd never have made it.'

'Reckoned on gettin' m'self a horse some place.'

'Not hereabouts, mister,' scoffed the woman. 'I got just one and he ain't for sale.' She glanced quickly at the rifle. 'What's yuh name?'

'Quinton—Frank Quinton.'

The woman nodded. 'Jessica Larson. I prefer just Jess. I ain't no Larson, not no more.'

'Yuh here alone, ma'am?' asked Quinton, letting his gaze move round the shadowed room. 'By y'self?'

'All by m'self,' said the woman sharply as she snatched the rifle back to her lap. 'But don't get no ideas I can't look to m'self just 'cus I'm a woman. I can do that very well.'

'Never doubted it, ma'am, not for a minute.' Quinton relaxed. 'Mite lonely ain't it?'

The woman stiffened. 'Depends. I prefer loneliness to what I had before.'

Was that the faintest twitch of a nerve in the woman's cheek, wondered Quinton, or a shift of the light. He shrugged. 'Free country,' he murmured.

'T'ain't,' snapped the woman. 'T'ain't that at all, not if yuh in a hell-prison. Yuh'd know that well enough.'

'Sure,' said Quinton darkly. 'Prison ain't no life of any sort, 'specially when yuh shouldn't be there. Even so, out here, alone—'

'Had a man here once. My husband, Sol. But he's dead now. Buried out back. Dug the grave m'self. Six feet of stinkin' dirt deep. Took a while, close on a week, but I figured it worth it. Wanted the sonofabitch deep as I could get him. Only place fittin' for a scumbag jailer, ain't it? Yuh'd go along with that, wouldn't yuh, mister? Yuh seen 'em.' The woman's fingers tightened on the rifle. The nerve in her cheek pulsed violently and her stare hardened to a glaze as bright as fresh ice. 'Still, it's done now, close on six months back. He ain't no jailer no more and I ain't his prisoner. Nossir!' Her eyes settled tight on Quinton's face. 'I shot the bastard.

Right here in this room.'

Quinton swallowed and was suddenly aware of the shadows closing in as if slipping like living things out of the walls.

'What's your story, mister?' smiled the woman softly. 'You have a jailer?'

Quinton told his story, quickly, briefly, and just as much of it as he chose to tell, without a single interruption from the woman, who simply stared at him through the telling, watching his eyes, the shift of his hands, until he was done. Then, in the strange silence they shared between them when it was over, the woman rose and crossed the room to the stove.

'Yuh'll be needin' to eat,' she said quietly. 'Best settle y'self for the night. Rest up. We'll talk some more come mornin'.'

About what, he pondered, when he was alone again, the woman asleep in a bunk far side of the room, the shadows still and gentler in the night's tight hug, and for what purpose?

Sure, the woman had saved his life, no doubting that, fed him, put a roof over his head for the night, but where did that leave him? Still without a horse, a gun, not least a decent pair of boots. Looked at from any angle, he was back where he started. Of course, he could maybe wait until the woman was sleeping real deep, sneak across the room, lift that Winchester from her side, go find her horse back of the homestead and ride out. Sure he could, but that would leave her stranded and defenceless. Hell, did it matter?

It mattered, he reckoned, because the odds of him coming back from Benefice to look to her and return what he had borrowed were a mite short.

He sighed and stared into the darkness. What sort of a woman was she, anyhow? She had offered no more in explanation of shooting her husband, but Quinton could figure it clear enough.

Sol Larson had doubtless promised all God's earth and more when he took her from some two-bit saloon, wedded her and brought her out here to this sand-drenched hell-hole. Give it a few months, the heat, the desert, the loneliness, and the place would have seemed a real prison. Short step from there to the beatings, the abuse ... Then snap, something had to give.

Quinton sighed again and closed his eyes. Say one thing for the woman, though, he thought, she was tough, not to be messed with, but what in hell sort of a future did she plan for herself? She had none here, not in a place like this, so where was the rest of her life heading?

Did she know?

She knew, and spelled it out in short, sharp statements of fact when Quinton stirred on the bed at the touch of first light.

'We're leaving,' she announced, standing stiffly over him. 'Soon as yuh quit that flea-pit. We ride double for the swing station at Kneebone. Takes about a day. Might be a chance of yuh pickin' up a horse there. That's your affair. Do as yuh please. There's clothes and a pair of Sol's boots out front. Try 'em on. Might fit. Then we go. Got it?'

'I got it,' said Quinton, blinking furiously. 'And what about y'self? What you plannin'?'

'That's my affair,' said the woman, and turned away.

'I should've known better than to ask,' murmured Quinton to himself.

SIX

Legget Rand reined his mount head-on for the cover of brush and sparse pine and came to a halt in the deepest of the shade. He shielded his gaze for a moment against the sun's fierce glare, wiped the sweat from his face, patted the snorting mount's neck, then relaxed through a long, grateful sigh.

He was still way ahead of Hooper's riders out of Benefice. That two hours' start out of town before first light had been worth the effort, and he reckoned he had got clear without being noticed. Fine, just fine, he thought, that was going to give him all the time and edge he needed—so long as he used it to good advantage.

And there lay his problem.

He was figuring on Hooper's men

holding tight to the main Jamesville trail for the rest of the day. They maybe reckoned they had little choice until they got at least a sighting of Quinton. But Quinton was never going to make it that easy. So what had he been doing since his release and what was he doing right now?

He would have been thrown out of Jamesville just as he stood, a ragbag of old clothes and worn boots, and left to fend for himself in the desert. Most men would turn up their toes within a day, but not Quinton. No, he would keep going somehow, and with Benefice his only objective he would head south.

Rand frowned and ran his hand thoughtfully over the mount's ears. South ... If Quinton had managed to get to water and bag himself a mount, he would be set dead-eyed for the swing station at Kneebone. Trouble being that water and a horse happening to be handy were in awful short supply out here. Only place he could think of ... But, no, grunted

56

Rand through his thoughts, not there, not Sol Larson's place. Larson would shoot a stranger soon as look at him. On the other hand, Quinton was a resourceful fellow. Supposing he had found what he needed at Larson's homestead—taken what he needed more like—and then supposing ...

Rand reined south-west. It was a long, hard ride to Kneebone. Best get started.

Willard Hooper was uneasy. The heat, the sand, the sweat, the jangle of tack, creak of leather were getting to him, slipping in and out of his nerve-ends like hot needles. Five days of this and he would be a wreck. Hell, would it take that long? Damn it, if six men needed all that time to gun just one, he had to be some man. And maybe he was. Nobody knew. Only thing they did know was that they had taken five years out of a man's life and the shame of it lay like a dead weight in their minds.

Hooper swallowed on his parched throat as the dust clouds swirled over the riders' heads. He should have stayed in town, he thought, left this whole mess for Luce Whitworth to settle. After all, it would be down to him come the final reckoning to finish the job. He was the real gun among them, maybe the only one with the cold eye for straight killing. Not Charlie, Jake, or them greenhorn deputies, least of all himself.

He swallowed again and choked on the dirt. Certainly not himself! He had wanted no part of the lynching that night, nothing to do with it. But he had been there at the kill, sure enough, swept up on the tide of hanging fever. Damn it, he should have known better. Should have seen that it would come to this. Too late now. Just too darned late ...

'We restin' up awhiles?' yelled out Charlie Piecemeal above the thud of hoofs. 'I'm gettin' sore!'

'Me too,' shouted Jake Mullen. 'We been ridin'—'

'I know how long we been ridin','

snapped Whitworth, 'and it ain't long enough. So settle yuh butts and keep goin'. Yuh stop when I say yuh stop, not before. Got it?'

Willard Hooper scowled to himself. See—see what is happening, he thought? It was getting to them all, and this soon. What would they be like come a whole day's riding? What after two, three days? If they lasted that long.

'So how come we know we're trailin' right, anyhow? Could be we got this all wrong. Could be Quinton's trailed way out east or mebbe he's gone deep south. Or mebbe he just ain't botherin'? Supposin' he figures on startin' afresh some place. Now that—'

'Will yuh shut yuh mouth, Jake Mullen. Shut it and hold it that way.' Luce Whitworth fixed the man with a tight, fierce glare, snapped the branch in his hands and threw the two halves into the flames of the fire. 'Yuh gettin' to be a real pain,' he croaked.

The others gathered round the glow at the mouth of the shallow creek kept their silence and went back to watching the dance of the blaze against the thick night sky.

'Even so,' murmured Charlie Piecemeal a few minutes later,' Jake's got a point there. We're spittin' on the wind a deal, ain't we? How many miles we done today, eh? Seems like hundreds judgin' by my butt! Bet it ain't more than a handful. And where, f'Crissake, are we really headin'? I wish somebody'd—'

'This is Luce's show,' growled Willard Hooper. 'Leave it to him.'

'It's every man's show,' said Jake, running his hands over his knees. 'We were all there that night, all sweatin' out heat and liquor, spooked up and spoilin' for somethin' to blow our heads on, and don't none of yuh say no other, 'cus it's fact. Plain fact. We all had a hand in the hangin'. We're all guilty as hell, and that makes this show—'

'Damn it, Jake, will yuh shut that crowin' mouth of yours!' snapped Whitworth.

'No, I'm darned if I will!' flared Jake, coming to his feet. 'I got as much right—'

'Cool it, Jake,' murmured Bob Sharman.

'Yeah, do just that,' echoed Vince Claim. 'Get some sleep or somethin'.'

'I ain't sleepin!' croaked Jake. 'Not t'night, not no night 'til this is all cleaned up proper and we get to thinkin' straight.'

'I'm tired of hearin' yuh, Jake,' said Hooper with a turn of his weary gaze.

'Well, mebbe yuh are,' flared Jake again. 'I couldn't give a cuss. Pay us all to stay awake, if yuh ask me, case that sonofabitch Quinton happens to be out there right now, skulkin' up on us, creepin' in like he was—'

'Jake,' soothed Charlie, 'this ain't the time.'

'Time? What the hell yuh talkin' of, Charlie Piecemeal?' spluttered Jake. 'It's always been *time*—time for a lynchin' and time to pay for it. And now we're payin' and goin' to keep on payin'—'

There was a sudden scuff of sand as Luce Whitworth sprang to his feet, lunged towards Jake Mullen and heaved the startled, open-mouthed fellow upright.

'Enough! D'yuh hear? Enough!' hissed the young sheriff, his eyes flashing anger, sweat dripping from his face. 'I ain't hearin' no more!'

The fist that thudded into Jake's face came with all the swirling speed and ferocity of a tornado and every last ounce of Whitworth's strength. Jake's stare was fixed and round and brilliantly white for just three seconds, a snip of time in which no one seemed to move, not even to breathe; only to sit there, silent and still as stone, and watch Jake's body leave the ground as if in flight and crash like a tossed sack of oats into a sprawl of rocks a dozen feet from the fire glow.

Charlie Piecemeal was the first to scramble to Jake's side, to put out a hand to the man's head and pull it back instantly at the touch of warm, sticky blood, then to peer closer beyond the sway of shadows into the grey lifeless face.

When he finally eased back on his knees and turned to face the others, Charlie's face was just as grey, almost as drained.

'He's dead, Luce,' he stammered. 'Yuh killed him, f'Crissake.'

And as if fanned by the chill of the moment, the flames leaped suddenly higher, fiercer, like the tongues of ghostly devils.

SEVEN

She must have been a good looker before all this, thought Quinton, watching the woman at the trickle of water through the parched creek stream. Shame Sol Larson had beaten the hell of it out of her. Maybe he had deserved to die.

Quinton eased his tired legs full stretch ahead of him on the rock shelf and studied the fit of his boots. A dead man's boots, he mused, narrowing his eyes, but real comfortable even so. Not much worn, neither. Same went for the pants and shirt. Sol had served his purpose!

He sighed, relaxed on his elbows and went back to watching the woman. She was going to be a problem if things did not go to plan at Kneebone. Just how did she figure he was going to pay for a horse, get himself some sidearms? She was hardly likely to make him a gift of her own mount and that Winchester she cradled like a babe. They were all that guaranteed her free passage. But to where? And why had she decided overnight to leave the homestead? Why with him, even to help him come to that?

She hadn't said, not so much as a word since they had ridden out of that hell-hole shack. Nothing, save to point the way once they were mounted up. But you could bet your sweet life she had it all figured. Sure to. She was that sort of a woman—decisive.

Quinton half smiled as he watched her scoop the cool water to her sweat and dirt-stained face. He bet that felt good; tempting enough to make her wish there was a flow fit to wash all over. He grunted. Now that ... And grunted again. He had been too long in Jamesville; too long with stinking scumbags and taunting guards; too damned long—with too much to think of.

His thoughts drifted for a moment, to Benefice, a man called Ben Little, a night of sultry heat; a rope, a noose, a gunned-down sheriff; townsfolk pointing accusative fingers, a marshal ... Jamesville. Hell, he should have ridden out of that devil town soon as the lynching was done, got clear, kept going. But his day was coming. Oh, yes, it was coming. The day when he would be there again, in that same street, with those same faces watching him. Only this time the fear would be in their eyes ...

'Yuh sweatin' some, mister,' said the woman, stepping over his outstretched legs. 'Yuh should get to the shade while yuh got the chance. Still some ways to go yet.'

'I been wonderin'—' began Quinton.

'Don't,' said the woman. 'T'aint worth the effort. Just do. And the doin' right now is gettin' to Kneebone. That's all there is. Yuh can wonder all yuh like after that.'

'And that's just what I—' began Quinton again.

'Save it. I ain't interested.'

The woman moved to the hitched mount and rummaged in a pannier. 'If it's a gun that's frettin' yuh, yuh got it,' she said, turning and tossing a holstered Colt and belt into Quinton's lap. 'Full loaded. Another piece of my husband you're welcome to. What yuh do with it is your affair. Yuh'll have to figure a horse y'self. Sol had only the one and that's mine.'

Quinton sighed. Like he had been thinking, the woman was the no-messing sort. And classy with it.

The swing station at Kneebone lay deep in a fold of the bare dirt hills, a silent, shadowed place marked only by the squat of rundown buildings, a drift of smoke and its sprawling corral.

An empty corral, noted Quinton, as he reined the mount into the spread of evening shade and felt the woman stiffen for a view at his back.

'Don't look to be too lively,' he murmured, shifting his gaze over the spread.

'Stage'll have been through days back,' said the woman. 'Another week before there's another. Old Pickins'll be restin up, bottle at his side.'

'Pickins?' queried Quinton.

'He runs the place. Been here a lifetime, and it shows.' The woman prodded a hand into Quinton's back. 'Move on. He ain't that liquored up not to have seen us. But go easy. He don't like nothin' sudden.'

Quinton urged the mount forward at a slow, steady pace, his gaze tight on the station where nothing moved among its shadowed darkness. No lantern lit, he pondered, not even at this hour. Maybe Pickins had done a shade too much resting up with that bottle!

He eased on the reins as they cleared the hills, felt the woman still stiff at his shoulders, the weight of the Colt at his waist. Its closeness was a help, save that the feel of it in his hand had been a strange, empty sensation. Five years was a long time to go without a firing. Time had been when he had reckoned he was fast, and faster than most, but now ... Hell, it might be weeks before he had a feel for it again and could shoot straight. Maybe the woman had figured that when she had tossed it to him. Figured he could do no harm for a while. And maybe she was right at that. But weeks he did not have. Benefice would not wait that long.

They came on into the shadows. Still nothing moved. Still only the silence and an emptiness that deepened the frown at Quinton's brow and darkened his stare 'til he seemed not to blink.

He reined the mount to a halt and sat without moving a muscle.

'What yuh stopped for?' asked the woman, laying a hand across his shoulder.

'Too damned quiet,' murmured Quinton.

'That's just Pickins. Sometimes gets to takin' a drop more than's good for him.'

'Mebbe, but does he get to takin' it in the dark?'

The woman sighed. 'Yuh gettin' jumpy, mister. Been cooped up too long in the Pen.'

Quinton grunted, clicked his tongue and rode the mount on, this time at no more than a walking pace. Cooped up maybe, he thought, but that tingle of sweat at his neck was no fool's whisper. That was real.

They rounded the empty corral and headed towards the front of the station. Quinton's stare had shifted now to the door and the blank, blind window alongside it. He was taking no odds at a movement at either one of them in the next minute. And no bets either on it being the booze-baffled Pickins.

He had brought the mount to within a reach of the hitching rail when he heard the creak from somewhere inside the station. The slide of a boot over a dry floorboard. Somebody edging closer to the door. Somebody who had been watching. The woman's hand slipped from his shoulder. He felt her tense, could feel the burn of her gaze on the silent station.

'Don't move,' he murmured.

They waited, staring, unmoving, the early night shadows snaking round them like a disturbed nest of vipers. And then the door swung open, slowly, creakily, on a dark blank space. Quinton's eyes narrowed, probing the darkness for the slightest movement, the shift of anything that resembled a body.

But it was a long time coming, almost a full half-minute before Quinton heard the sound of a footfall, saw the blur of legs easing to the faint light until the full shape of the man filled the doorway, the glint of a rifle barrel fixing the new arrivals where they sat.

'Closed for the night,' croaked the man ahead of spitting into the dirt. 'Unless, o'course, yuh got no place else to go, and there ain't no place boastin' a roof. So what'll it be?'

Quinton's gaze moved over the man like a beam. Gunslinger for sure, he reckoned; youngish, brittle-eyed and full of his self-esteem, leastways while he had that rifle tight in his hands. But not alone, he thought. No, this fellow had back up, somebody standing to his side. Where, damn it?

The answer to that came in the thud of another footfall as a second, stockier, older man pushed the youngster aside and framed himself against the dark interior. Similar cut to this fellow, thought Quinton; gunslinger, deal more experienced, meaner, hungrier look in his eyes, twisted slant to his lips, thumbs hooked lazily in his belt.

'Where's Pickins?' snapped the woman suddenly. 'What yuh done with him?'

'Well, now,' said the older man, 'I'd guess yuh'd say he's sleepin' things off. Sorta nursin' a sore head.'

The younger man giggled. 'Yeah, yuh'd say that—among other things,' he grinned.

'If you've—' began the woman.

'No, lady, we're goin' to let the old stager live outa the goodness of our hearts.' The stocky man leaned on the door jamb. 'See, we kinda need him for a while, just 'til we figure it safe for us to move on. While we hole-up quiet like against any mule-headed lawmen sittin' on our tails. Day or so, that's all.' The man's eyes gleamed. 'Time to get to know yuh better, ma'am. My pleasure, I'm sure.' His partner giggled again. 'Though we do seem to be gettin' a mite overcrowded here, and that horse of yours is sure as hell lookin' weighed down with the pair of yuh aboard. So I guess the answer is to cut down the numbers, eh? Make life a whole lot easier, for the horse, and fairer when it comes to sharin' yuh round, ma'am.'

And then the man's hand slid to his holstered Colt as if reaching for another drink.

EIGHT

The sweat in Quinton's neck had been close to boiling when his blood ran suddenly cold and calm through his veins and he knew instinctively what he had to do if he was going to take another breath that shadow-filled night.

He reined the mount tight on an ear-splitting yell that spooked the horse high and pawing on the chilling air, at the same time throwing the woman to the ground where she squirmed away like a whipped snake. A cloud of dust covered Quinton as he dived from the mount, his Colt firm in his hand and already blazing when he hit the dirt, took a deep breath and sprang to his feet again, another spitting roar of lead ripping into the doorway.

He heard a gurgling groan, saw a spurt

of blood fan over the gloom like a spray of burning stars and weaved forward for a sight of the rifle barrel.

The younger man had backed against the station wall, his fingers in one moment tightening, in the next loosening on the weapon as he stared wild-eyed and wet with fear at the mayhem erupting around him.

He was shaking, fumbling at the rifle trigger, his mouth opening and closing on pathetic gulps and splutters when Quinton came face-on to him, paused a second, his eyes dark as craters, lips tight as ridge rock, then carefully, deliberately, fired two shots clean into the gunslinger's head and watched him crumple, twitch once and stay very still with his dead stare wide to the night.

Quinton merely grunted when it was done, then slid the Colt back to its holster as natural as taking breath.

'Heard it all from in here, every last shot

and rasp of it, but I'd sure as hell given a lot to have seen it—seen them mangy scum go down like the dogs they were.' The old man shifted the lantern closer to him where he sat at the long, scrubbed table, poured himself another finger of whiskey, and offered the bottle to Quinton and the woman.

'Rode in at a lick soon after noon,' the man went on, slapping his lips round the flavour of the drink. 'Never clapped eyes on the devils before, and never got to hearin' their names neither, but I could see what they were straight up—gunslingers. And in some trouble, too, I'd reckon. Anyhow, never got to that. Never had the chance. They trussed me up real good right here, scattered the half-dozen horses from the corral, whipped me some outa sheer spite, then sat back. I figured they were holin'-up and keepin' low against somebody hummin' on their tails. No tellin' how long they'd have stayed, but no doubtin' what they had in mind for me when they were all through. Yuh not happened by, mister, I'd have been crow meat come sun-up. That would've been the end of old Pickins and no mistake.'

The man finished his drink, sat back and stared hard at Quinton. 'That must've been some shootin' out there,' he said quietly. 'Real fast. Had to be. Nothin' else would've done.' He leaned forward again, his tired eyes narrowing. 'Your name Quinton by any chance?' he asked.

Quinton leaned away from the window, glanced quickly at the woman, and smiled softly at the man. 'The very same,' he said. 'How'd yuh know?'

Pickins relaxed again. 'Figured so. Stage came through a week ago. Driver said as how the word was yuh were comin' out and in a none-too-happy mood. Talk was yuh'd be ridin' hard for Benefice. Settle a few scores. We all heard about what happened there. Can't say I blame yuh. Fact is, though, mister, they're goin' to know all over that two-bit town by now that you're out and headin' their way. Yuh reckoned on that?'

No, thought Quinton, he had not, leastways not that the news would be out so soon.

'Gives them an edge, don't it?' the old man went on. 'Kinda prepares them for your arrival. Means they'll be ready. Just waitin'.' He sighed. 'Still, what I seen of yuh, and judgin' by them sonsofbitches stiffenin' out there, I'd reckon the odds about equal.' He turned to the woman, where she sat in a shadowed corner of the room. 'Meantime, how come you're with this fella, Jess? Where's Sol? How's he doin' these days? Whole year and more since I seen him.'

'Sol ain't around no more,' said the woman sharply. Then, with a glance at Quinton, added, 'He went West some place. I ain't seen him since.'

Pickins ran a hand over his stubbled chin. 'Always was a strange one,' he said thoughtfully. 'Never any figurin' him.

Livin' out there like he did, then draggin' yuh into it. Yuh mebbe best shut of him, Jess. Don't say it lightly, but facts is facts.' He sighed again and yawned. 'You folks are welcome to the place for as long as it suits. Just help y'selves. Me, I'm for turnin' in. Got one helluva sore head here!' He came to his feet and turned to Quinton. 'Thanks again, mister. I'm in yuh debt, deep as it gets.'

Quinton nodded and smiled. 'My pleasure,' he murmured.

'Yeah,' said the old man, shuffling away to his bed, 'I figured so.'

The night was deep and still and silent when the woman came to Quinton's side at the open doorway and stood there for a moment taking in the chill fresh air. 'Pickins was right,' she said quietly without looking at him. 'Yuh proved somethin' t'night, didn't yuh? Proved yuh could still handle a gun for one; proved yuh could kill for another. That feel better?'

Quinton's gaze stayed steady on the empty land. 'No, ma'am, can't say it does. Just proves the odds stay even when it comes to survivin'. I ain't askin' for more.'

'Yuh still goin' on to Benefice?' she asked.

'That's my plan. Always has been. Got m'self a horse now. Them gunslingers had hitched their mounts out back. Horse, gun, that's as much as I need.'

'I wish yuh well,' said the woman. 'Mebbe we'll meet up again some place.'

'Yuh stayin' here?'

'No, I'll mebbe head West in a day or so. Go make m'self a fresh start somewhere.'

Quinton grunted. 'I'm grateful to yuh for your help, ma'am. Wouldn't have made it this far without yuh.'

'And mebbe I wouldn't be goin' free if yuh'd said to Pickins back there as to where my husband really is. Thanks.'

'Yuh could have shot me, too, 'stead of near drownin' me! Why didn't yuh?

Chance was clear enough.'

The woman stepped to the edge of the darkness. 'I don't know,' she said. 'Should have done. Save yuh gettin' y'self killed when yuh hit Benefice.' She turned and stared at him. ' 'Cus yuh will, mister—goddamn—Quinton. Shot and spewin' on dirt sure as there'll be first light in a few short hours. T'aint a healthy prospect.'

And then she brushed past him without another word, back into the room and the shadowed corner where she would sleep.

Say this for the woman, thought Quinton, still watching the night, she never said nothing short of what was on her mind. Straight up, straight out, no messing.

Trouble was, she could be right.

NINE

They were digging graves at the swing station at Kneebone when Legget Rand finally had the place in view at first light.

Old Pickins and a woman heaving away at the dirt far side of the corral in an effort to go deep enough before full sun-up. Now, just what in tarnation ... Rand sat his mount quiet for a moment watching the diggers, a frown already creeping across his brow. Unless he was much mistaken the woman out there was Jess Larson. How come she was here, he wondered, but a darn sight more to the point, who in hell were they burying?

Rand brought his weary mount out of the foothills at a steady gallop, his gaze hard on the diggers until the thudding of his approach halted their efforts and they rested on their shovels.

'Darn me if it ain't Legget Rand,' wheezed Pickins, mopping his brow. 'Seems like half the territory's on the move—all on account of Quinton, yuh can bet. Well, he's too late by a good coupla hours.' He grinned at the woman. 'Guess we can't do more than offer him coffee, eh, ma'am?'

'And explain just what the hell we're doin' diggin' two fresh graves.'

'That'll be all my pleasure, ma'am,' smiled Pickins. 'Every last detail. Yeah ...' He threw aside his shovel and climbed out of the hole. 'Mornin', Mister Rand,' he called. 'And just what brings yuh this way? Trouble?'

Charlie Piecemeal's guts were twisting in on themselves; knotting up until it seemed they would burst clean through his pants. Hell, it took some swallowing to think of Jake getting himself killed like that, and for no good reason save that he had been all spooked up and could never hold his tongue. Darned fool! But that was no excuse for Luce Whitworth breaking out like he had—like he always did more like. Never could rope his temper long enough to take breath. One of these days somebody was going to be a jump ahead of him, and that day was maybe not so far away judging by the way things were going.

Charlie spat into the dirt and tightened his grip on the reins. Just where were they trailing now, he wondered? Still vaguely north best he could figure, but vague it surely was. Could go on like this for weeks and still without a sight of Quinton. Sonofabitch could be anywhere—out there skulking in the rocks, hidden in the brush, snuggled down in the boulders, riding clear some place on the plains' horizon. No knowing. Or maybe he was trailing them, coming up on their butts like a long shadow ready to pick them off whenever he chose. That sounded more Quinton's style.

He spat again and grunted. Not that Whitworth and Hooper seemed to figure it that way. They just kept going, straight on, as if up ahead was all the land there was. Hooper knew no better. He might be the smart one back there at his fancy saloon, skimming down the whiskey, marking the cards when he chose, smiling sweet as candy at his girls, but out here was different. Here, he was no better, no smarter than the next man and, seeing him up there tight as a tick at Whitworth's side, relying entirely on that frenzy-headed sheriff and his greenhorn sidekicks, Hooper was going to be about as useful as a spokeless wheel when the chips were down.

Might have been a deal saner to have ridden back to Benefice soon as they had buried Jake. And he would have, save for the way folks would have seen it. Charlie Piecemeal was no quitter. Nossir. But he was getting awful close to thinking like one.

And so Charlie might have gone on

thinking had it not been for the sudden blur of movement way out on the bluff to his right. Could have been anything, of course, he thought, reining back; some wild animal, shift of the light, his imagination. Or it could just as easily have been a lone rider, somebody trailing right alongside them, who knew they were there and was content enough for now to simply watch.

Maybe they should go take a closer look, just to be sure. Or maybe he should go do the looking himself, leave Hooper and Whitworth out of it. Hell, it needed somebody to do something!

And with that Charlie Piecemeal broke the trail and headed for the bluff.

'So that's the way of it,' said Legget Rand, throwing the dregs of his coffee to the sand. 'Yuh ain't done Quinton no favours lettin' him go like that. 'Bout now he's ridin' clean into a blaze of guns that'll go on roarin' 'til he's down and dead. And there ain't nothin' we can do about it.'

'Well,' said Pickins slowly, 'that's as mebbe. Tell yuh somethin', though, there weren't no way of holdin' him here, leastways not that I'd have cared to try. Man's got a mind of his own, Legget, and who can blame him? Not been for that leg of yours, yuh'd mebbe have done somethin' similar. Quinton'll go where Quinton wants, and do just as he wants for as long as it takes. And that's the way of it too.'

Rand sighed. 'You're right. Too darned right. Hell, if I'd got here last night 'stead of restin' up—'

'T'ain't too late as I see it,' said Jess Larson, scuffing the toe of her boot through a scattering of pebbles.

'How come?' asked Rand.

'Fella won't have gotten too far yet. And he'll stay clear of the main trail. We could ride out, give him a hand.'

'We?' frowned Pickins.

'Sure,' said the woman. 'Me and Rand here. Least we can do.'

'Yuh'd do that? Damnit, lady, we're talkin' here of—' began Rand.

'I know what we're talkin' of, mister, and I also seen what Quinton did here last night with them scumbag gunslingers. But two guns is one thing; six ain't one mite a fair fight. Fella needs somebody to stand to him, and I don't see nobody but us, you and me, do you? Assumin', o' course, yuh got the stomach for it.'

'Have you?' croaked Rand.

'Try me,' said the woman.

'Yeah,' smiled Pickins, 'try her.'

Charlie Piecemeal reckoned he was seeing things. Getting senile and in sore need of spectacles. Nothing else for it. There was about as much movement out here in this scrub and brush and dirt-land as there was in an empty bottle. Not so much as a fly buzzing.

Still, that was no excuse for Vince Claim to come nosying after him like he was rounding up a loose steer. He watched the deputy approaching from the main trail for a moment, then eased his mount on to the cover of a mound of boulders. Give the fellow something to do, he thought, let him come find me! He smiled softly to himself. Bit of a diversion would whip up Luce Whitworth's blood for a while; maybe make him realize that not everybody was at his beck and call. Some folk had their own way of going about things.

Even so, he was a mite sore at being fooled like that. Could have sworn he saw a movement out on the bluff. Not like him to make a mistake like that, but in this heat, in these circumstances, fellow could get to seeing and thinking all manner of things. That had been Jake's trouble—too much sun boiling up back of his head. Poor devil ...

He shifted in the saddle, listening for a sound of the deputy. Fellow was taking his time. Goddamnit, what did he need, a smoke signal! He sighed and relaxed again. Typical, he thought, you couldn't even rate Whitworth's choice of deputies. Take Vince ... Fast with a gun maybe, and useful with his fists, but when it came to thinking—a head full of yesterday's sawdust. And Bob Sharman was hardly a deal brighter. Sharman's idea of deputizing was displaying his fancy handiwork with them twin Colts of his. Not a pinch of sense otherwise.

Charlie cleared the sweat from his face. But, hell, both Vince and Bob had been keen enough that night of the lynching. Nothing cluttering their minds when they helped put the noose around Ben Little's neck. Sharp enough then, and no remorse neither. But maybe they were thinking other thoughts right now. Thinking of Quinton coming back, where he was, what he was planning ...

And just where in tarnation was that fool deputy?

Charlie eased his mount out of the cover and scanned the scrub. Not a sight, not a sound of the fellow. He gone and got himself lost or something, he wondered? And where were the others skulking? Must have moved on down the trail. Well, Vince Claim could go on wandering all he liked. More fool him. Maybe some rattler out here would have him for supper!

Charlie moved on, back to the trail. Now might be the time to turn tail and head for Benefice. Do it before Whitworth got to missing him. But, hell, no, that would be no way of settling things. Charlie Piecemeal was not for running out on nobody. Not in his nature.

But it was in Charlie's nature for his blood to run cold when he saw the loose mount trot out of the brush ahead of him, the body of Vince Claim thrown across it. And run colder still when he saw the rope noosed tight at his neck.

TEN

The roll of thunder heaved deep in the bank of dark cloud to the north to break Legget Rand's concentration on the dusty trail. Bad weather moving in and heading their way, he thought, glancing quickly at the woman reining her mount easy a length behind him. That was all they needed: poor light, heavy rain, tracks washed clean away, and night settling early. Even the gods were siding with Quinton. Well, maybe they had their priorities right.

'Not so good,' he called, pointing up ahead to the thickening cloud. 'We'll need to clear this flat land soon as we can. Get into the hills. Quinton'll be in there somewhere.'

Jess Larson firmed her hat tighter on her head and turned up the collar of her jacket. 'Yeah,' she answered, 'and so will the others. Mebbe he's spotted them by now.'

'Or they him,' said Rand.

The woman's gaze darkened. 'I gotta deal more faith in Quinton than you appear to have, Mister Rand,' she called above the strengthening wind.

'Good. He's goin' to need all he can get.'

'He's nobody's fool,' she called again. 'I can vouch for that.'

'Sure he's not. And there's six men up there desperate to cut out their past. They're no fools neither, especially Luce Whitworth.'

The woman was silent for a moment. 'Yuh reckon Quinton'll make it?'

'Make what? He's already signed up to his fate, ma'am. Signed and settled. All it needs now is for somebody to deliver it. And they will, if not sooner, then surely later. Don't much matter.'

'I don't see it that way, Mister Rand.'

You, lady, may very well not, thought Rand, but then you were not in Benefice that night, and you are hardly likely to have a clear notion of just how far men will go when they see the future coming up black as them hills ahead of us. There are no limits drawn and none considered. Survival, lady, survival ...

Or maybe Jess Larson knew a deal more about survival than he gave her credit for. She was keeping awful quiet about what had happened to her husband. Not that it was anybody's business save hers. But survival would have been high on the list of the daily round when it came to living with Sol, and Jess, he reckoned, had learned fast. Would have had to, and it had sure as hell taken it out of her. She needed time and some place quiet to get back to being a real woman. So how did she plan on doing that, he wondered?

Not this way, that was for certain! She had maybe ridden out of one hell, but that was no good reason to go looking for another that was not of her making and where the survival chances were a darned sight slimmer. And yet there had been no persuading her either. Not a hope. If she figured she owed Quinton some for gunning those scumbags at Kneebone, she was determined to pay back in full. He could just not fathom why ...

'Rain's gettin' close,' she shouted above the sudden whip of the wind.

Too right it was, thought Rand—along with the rest of the storm around Quinton.

Willard Hooper backed deeper into the cover of the rock overhang, squinted against the lash of the cold, stinging rain and began to shiver. This was going to be about the last throw of the dice as far as he was concerned. Soon as the weather cleared, he was calling it a day, heading back to Benefice, face whatever he had to face on his own patch and to hell with it.

Jake Mullen's death had been bad enough, something that should never have happened, but the killing of Vince in that way had turned his guts to ice. And it was no good trying to shy clear of who had done it: Quinton, right under their darned noses. He was out there now, sitting like a scrawny vulture on the edge of their shadows, watching them, just waiting on the next chance to move in for another killing. Hell, it was like listening to the undertaker hammer up your own coffin!

He shivered again and glanced quickly over the faces of the others. No need for a long look. How they felt was clear as moons in their eyes—all, that is, save for Luce Whitworth. He just squatted there, polishing and fingering his Colt like it was some hungry hound straining on the leash of his fingers. You could bet he could hardly wait to get to using it and was already planning just how much lead he would pump into Quinton when the time came. Always assuming he got within spitting distance of the fellow.

Bob Sharman was not so certain. Seeing

Vince like that had chilled him through, set him to wondering that maybe he should not have been so keen to ride alongside Luce on this venture, that maybe it was all one big mistake which had gone wrong from the start and was getting worse. Might have been a darn sight saner to have stayed in Benefice. Now, the real doubt was, would he see the place again?

Charlie Piecemeal was a mess. He had the look of a man who had not only seen a ghost but felt the touch of it. He had not stopped shaking since trailing Vince's body out of the scrub to the main trail. There could hardly be a bone in his body not rattling loose. 'Just look at this, will yuh? Just look,' was all he had been able to mouth, over and over again. It had taken a slap across the face from Luce to shut him up. When it came to moving again, it would be as much as they could do to get the wreck aboard his mount.

'Soon as the weather eases some, we go higher,' said Whitworth, spitting into a pool of rainwater. 'Up into them rocks there. Give ourselves a clearer view.'

'Quinton ain't goin' to make himself that easy to spot,' murmured Sharman. 'He ain't that stupid.'

' 'Course he ain't,' grinned Whitworth, 'but he's gotta move. Can't stay out here forever.'

The deputy shrugged deeper into his jacket. 'Mebbe we should pull out now while we got the chance. Get ourselves back to town.'

'Yuh can swallow that sorta talk, Bob Sharman,' snapped Whitworth. 'We ain't pullin' out to nowhere. We'll get that sonofabitch, see if we don't.'

'Bob's mebbe talkin' sense,' said Hooper, without looking at the sheriff. 'I ain't for bein' stalked like some animal. We get back to town we got more folk standin' with us.'

'Yuh figure Quinton's goin' to let us do that—ride out, all quiet and peaceable?' sneered Whitworth. ' 'Course he ain't.

He'll be on to us before we gone a mile. F'get it. We go after him. Yuh got it? What yuh say, Charlie; we go string up that scumbag?'

Charlie Piecemeal shivered, his teeth chattering like loose stones in an empty can.

'Charlie?' grunted Whitworth. 'Yuh hearin' me?'

'Loud and goddamn clear,' hissed Charlie, rocking on his heels where he squatted in the darkness at the back of the overhang. 'And yuh spoutin' fool talk. We ain't got no chance. Quinton's got us, just like he said he would day that marshal dragged him off to Salton. He said it, I heard him—heard him clear as I'm hearin' him now.'

Bob Sharman shuddered. Willard Hooper sweated.

Whitworth spun the chamber of his Colt. 'Yuh spooked up, yuh darned fool!' he cursed. 'Half a mind to put yuh out your misery right now.'

'Yeah, yuh do that,' said Charlie, flaring suddenly. 'Yuh do just that—clean and fast, no messin'. Do it before Quinton marks me out for next on his list. Or mebbe it'll be you, Luce. Yuh thought of that? Could be he's got yuh dead-eye centre of his sights right now.'

Whitworth aimed the barrel of the Colt at Charlie's head. 'Any more talk like that and I swear I'll finish yuh, Charlie, just like you're askin' for.'

Willard Hooper turned his gaze back to the darkness, the lash of rain, and listened to the thunder rolling through the hills like the growl of a ranting giant. How long would Quinton give them before he came to finish it, he wondered?

Who would see him first?

ELEVEN

They dragged through the beat of the rain, the snap and snarl of the wind, until they were drenched and black as ragged old crows. Silent too; not a word passed between them as Rand and the woman made their slow, sodden way from the flat lands out of Kneebone to the lower reaches of the hills.

Rand had long since given up any hope of following Quinton's early tracks from the station. All he had beneath him now was a fast thickening swirl of mud, and all he could see up ahead was the darkness of the storm merging with the gathering depths of the night. Some mixture, he thought, reining his mount against another slither. Time to call it a day, hole up some place dry as they could find and sit out the storm to first light. He guessed Quinton would be doing much the same. But what of Hooper, Whitworth and their boys? How far had they come and where were they now? Watching for Quinton or still unaware of him?

He urged his mount through a gap in the bulge of rock, waited a moment to be certain the woman was following, then pushed on hurriedly for the sweep and roll of dark boulders to his right. Maybe there was some shelter among them, a small cave, hollowed-out place beneath an overhang—anywhere, damn it, where they could get clear of the relentless lash of rain and put their backs to the whip of the wind. Chances were, he reckoned, that Jess Larson was getting close to exhaustion. Last thing he wanted was a sick woman to look to.

They stumbled into the shelter at the foot of a sudden mud-slicked slope. Not much of a place, thought Rand, dismounting at the mouth of the hollow, but the overhang was broad and the ground a deal firmer and dry. Best they could do for now.

'Far as we go, ma'am,' he called to the woman. 'Get y'self in here while I hitch the mounts and bring us some blankets. No hope of lightin' a fire 'til this weather eases. Just have to manage.'

Twenty minutes later they were seated as deep into the hollow as they could go, wrapped in blankets, fighting off their bouts of shivering, and watching the darkness as if expecting it to part like a curtain on some sunlit dawn.

'Goin' to be a long night,' croaked Rand, as he wiped the last of the rain from his face. 'Try sleepin' some if yuh can. Ain't a deal else we can do.'

'Yuh figure Quinton's out there?' asked the woman.

'He's there, ma'am, holed up much like us if he's got any sense. He'll wait for first light.'

The woman flashed an anxious glance at Rand. 'Then what? Mebbe he ain't crossed those fellas huntin' him. Mebbe he'll ride slap into them. Won't be much of a chance for him then.'

Rand grunted. 'I don't see Quinton doin' nothin' foolhardy as that, ma'am. He's had five years to figure this, see all the angles, rate all the things that might happen. Kinda like watchin' dust settle—and I bet he ain't missed one speck.'

The woman shivered again and pulled her blanket closer. 'What yuh goin' to do when we find him?' she murmured.

'That, ma'am, is goin' to be difficult,' sighed Rand. 'Best I can hope for is to stop him ridin' into Benefice, save him getting himself killed. Most I'll get is a sore head for my trouble! Still, it's worth a try.' He sighed again. 'Trouble is, Quinton's seein' and feelin' only one thing: revenge. That's all he's seen and felt those years. Prison gets to yuh like that.'

The woman was silent for a moment. 'Yeah,' she said at last, 'I know,' then closed her eyes on something only she could see.

Rand waited a long, cold hour for Jess Larson to drift into sleep before easing himself back to the mouth of the shelter. Wind was dying some, he thought, and the cloud bank beginning to break. Storm would have passed by first light. Maybe then would be the time to urge the woman to head back to Kneebone, forget Quinton, just keep out of the whole mangy affair. She had no part of it, not the lynching, not now. Only misfortune she had crossed was meeting up with Quinton back there at the homestead.

He frowned. That was troubling him too. Just what had happened there, and how come ...?

But that was as far as Rand's pondering went as he turned, slow and easy, at the sound of a slip of loose rock behind him, the slither of what might have been a footfall through mud, and then the sharp click of the hammer pulled back on a Colt.

Rand made no move, not so much as a blink as he peered into the darkness waiting for the shape of the man to step through it. He swallowed, wondering now if he would ever get to see who it was out there or only hear him, the blaze of a shot that would bring its own darkness.

Silence save for the moan of the dying wind, the soft beat of rain. But was that the slide of a shadow, the blurred shift of something, somebody passing? Had he seen it before, in that room above the saloon at Benefice; that same shape, tall and dark?

Sure he had—only this was no haunting. This was for real.

'I reckon this is goin' to be our day,' grinned Luce Whitworth, lifting his face to the clear blue sky and the shimmering glare of the sun. 'Yeah, our day, all the way.' He closed his eyes for a moment, relished the fresh air and warmth at his skin, then settled his hat firm on his head and turned sharply to stare at the others. 'Don't yuh fellas reckon so?' he asked. 'Don't yuh feel it deep in yuh bones? Day we get to Quinton, finish him and ride for home?'

Willard Hooper groaned inwardly. All he was feeling right now was a mouth as foul as a rattler's shed skin, limbs as heavy and dead as sodden logs, and a herd of spooked longhorns thundering through his head. Last thing he wanted to hear at this hour, in his state, was fool talk about taking Quinton.

Bob Sharman blinked and swallowed and listened to the creak and crack of his bones as he stretched. Damn it, he could use a soft bed and the home comforts that went with it. Hadn't felt so stiff and stale since liquoring up for three days at Hanks Woods's wedding feast. As for Quinton ... Who gave a spit on the wind any more? Fellow could go to hell as far as he was concerned and he guessed Charlie Piecemeal was feeling much the same.

But Charlie Piecemeal was feeling very little at that moment—only seeing things: the blood oozing from Jake Mullen's head, the blown eyes and bloated tongue of Vince Claim strung out across his mount, a blurred shape moving through the sunbaked rocks, or was it a ghost? Or was he going stark raving mad? Maybe he was there already.

'Well, fellas, what'd yuh say?' grinned Whitworth again. 'This goin' to be our day?'

'Make of it what yuh will, Luce,' croaked Hooper, 'I'm pullin' out. This is town folks' business and they'll have to settle it best they can when Quinton rides in.'

'Yuh goin' no place, Willard,' snapped Whitworth. 'None of yuh. There'll be no pullin' out. Yuh hear me?'

'Sure we hear yuh, Luce,' began Sharman, 'but, hell, we ain't gettin' nowheres, and if yuh ask me—'

'I ain't,' snapped Whitworth again, his

fingers skimming the butt of his Colt. 'I'm tellin' yuh.'

'You're out-voted, Luce,' said Hooper. 'We head back to Benefice and that's an end of it.'

'While we're still breathin',' added Sharman.

Hooper grunted. Sharman swallowed. Charlie Piecemeal stared for a moment into nowhere then slowly, silently, turned his back on Whitworth and walked away to the rocks.

'Where yuh think yuh goin', Charlie?' called Whitworth. 'Yuh get y'self back here.'

'He's plumb brain-cracked,' murmured Sharman.

'He'll sure as hell be just that time I'm through with him!' hissed Whitworth. 'Charlie—yuh get back here right now.'

'Leave him, Luce,' said Hooper. 'We'll round him up when we're ready to pull out.'

'There'll be no pullin' out,' flared

Whitworth, stepping aside as he drew his Colt. 'And I'll down the next man who mouths it.'

'Hold it,' clipped Hooper, beginning to sweat. 'This ain't gettin' us no place. We gotta think clear.'

'That's just what we gotta do,' stammered Sharman.

'And I'm doin' it,' snarled Whitworth.

'Not that way yuh ain't,' began Hooper again. 'All we're doin' right now is wastin' time and givin' Quinton the edge he needs. We pull out now, we can be near as damnit home come nightfall. Then, and only then, we get to sortin' this proper—which is what we should've done in the first place.'

'Makes good sense to me,' agreed Sharman. 'Like Willard here says, we gotta—'

'To hell with yuh!' sneered Whitworth. 'There'll be no pullin' out, yuh hear, no pullin' out. We started this, we finish it, out here, no place else.' He gestured with the Colt. 'Now get y'selves mounted up and cut the talkin'. We're goin' to find Quinton and do just as we agreed. Got it?'

'Don't look like Charlie's comin' with us,' said Sharman, as Charlie Piecemeal reined his mount into view. 'I'd say Charlie's all through here.'

'Yuh dead right he is,' snapped Whitworth before spitting into the dirt ahead of him and tightening his grip on the Colt.

'No!' yelled Hooper.

But his cry was no more than a whisper against the roar of Luce Whitworth's rapid shots.

TWELVE

Jess Larson flinched at the blaze of the shots and the echoing whine of them through the heat-cloaked hills. Legget Rand reined up tight ahead of her and calmed his bucking mount to a halt. 'Somewhere down there,' he called to the woman. 'Far side of the dry creek.'

'Quinton?' she asked, patting her horse's neck.

'Mebbe. Him, or that Benefice mob.'

'We get down there, take a look?'

'Not yet,' said Rand. 'Hold to this track awhiles. See what happens.'

Damn, thought the woman as the mount eased, snorted and sweated, just typical of a fellow like Rand. Too cautious by a mile. Maybe more concerned about that weakened leg of his than somebody needing help. What the hell good was it going to do sitting up here when Quinton was maybe pinned down under fire? Could be he was surrounded; half-a-dozen guns all set to blaze lead minute he so much as blinked. And who was to say he had not been hit, maybe bleeding best part of his guts to the dirt?

Not Legget Rand! No, he was going to just sit it out and wait. Waiting never got nobody nowhere when it came to hitting back. She knew that well enough. You had to act, or never have the chance. Just like she had that day when Sol had stripped her naked, beaten her near senseless. She had acted then and no mistake; crawled her way to that rifle of his, taken it, hugged it to her, and then ...

Now that had been hitting back, hard as it comes, no messing. That was how you had to be when things got really rough. And this, she reckoned, was as rough as she cared to see it get ...

'Darnit, woman, what in hell's name yuh

doin'?' yelled Rand as his mount bucked again under Jess Larson's wild-eyed dash for the slope to the creek.

But it was too late then. She was gone like a bullet from a gun—and probably heading straight into the real thing, thought Rand, through a long, despairing groan.

Bob Sharman simply stood, swaying slightly, his face as grey as the dirt at his feet, his gaze riveted on the sprawled dead body of Charlie Piecemeal. Willard Hooper's eyes were narrowed, tight as hairline cracks through an ancient rock, an oozing sweat trickling from his brow to his cheeks. His fingers twitched only once, as if about to reach for the gun beneath his jacket, then were still and hanging like dried weeds.

'Yuh fool,' he croaked in a voice that seemed to crawl from his mouth. 'Yuh darned, pea-brained fool. Yuh had no good reason—'

'He was wastin' on us,' snapped Whitworth. 'Goin' out of his mind. We ain't got no place for that kinda body.'

'We were six when we left Benefice,' said Hooper softly. 'Now, look—half of us gone and as far from Quinton as we ever were. What yuh thinkin' of, Luce? Just what the hell we doin' out here save for diggin' our own graves? We all goin' mad or somethin'?'

A nerve began to jump like a trapped tick in Whitworth's cheek and for a split second there was uncertainty in the dance of his eyes, the grip on his Colt, the shifting shrug and nudge at his shoulders. 'We still got only one thing to do,' he drawled. 'Just get to Quinton before—'

Hooper, Sharman, Whitworth all stiffened at the sudden clatter of loose rocks, the tumble of stones, beat of hoofs and snort of the mount as Jess Larson tumbled from the slope to the bed of the creek.

She might then have realized she had read this all wrong; that Quinton was not here, never had been, and that the shots she had thought meant for him had killed the fellow already gathering flies. She might, too, have had a half-chance then to kick her mount into new life and spring clear of the startled men surrounding her, leave them bewildered and open-mouthed in a cloud of dust behind her. But the rush of the dash down the slope, the bucking, prancing, slithering weight of the horse beneath her had been too much for her to handle so that she had finally lost her grip on the flying reins and was dumped like spare baggage to the ground.

And there, spitting dust and dirt, her hair scattered across her shoulders as if at the eye of a hurricane, she sat watching Luce Whitworth move towards her, a slow, sneering grin already twisting at his lips.

'If this ain't the heavens openin'?' he croaked, standing over the woman. 'Look yuh here, Willard. Look what we just landed ourselves. Ain't we in real luck? Didn't I say that?'

'Where the hell she come from, f'Crissake?' hissed Sharman, coming closer.

'Don't matter none, does it?' grinned Whitworth.

'All that matters is she's here and I reckon I can figure why.'

Jess Larson spat, glared, tossed her head and shuffled back on her butt through the dirt.

'Sol Larson's wife,' said Hooper darkly. 'I seen her before. Lives out that flea shack edge of the desert.'

'Well, now,' murmured Whitworth, 'that kinda fits the picture, don't it? I'd reckon on Quinton havin' found her and brought her along for the company, wouldn't you? Yeah, just that, and now he's gone and got careless and lost her. Ain't that the size of it, lady? Am I figurin' it right? Oh, yes, I reckon so. My, my ... Well, that's real dandy for us, 'cus now we got an edge that's goin' to bring Quinton scuttlin' out of them rocks like a lizard in a frenzy. Yessir ...'

The woman stayed silent, glaring and defiant, and made no move save to spit again, clean on to Luce Whitworth's boot.

Legget Rand shuffled through the hot dirt until he was tight in the sprawl of rocks, cleared the sweat from his face, took a deep breath and risked raising his head above the line of cover.

He had an uncluttered view from here down the slope to the bed of the creek, could see exactly where Jess Larson had come to grief and been thrown from her mount, and was in no doubt of the identity of the three men standing over her. But why only three, he wondered? Where were the others? It had been resolved firm enough that night in the saloon that six men would ride out from Benefice to face Quinton. Six had been chosen; six had readied up for the start at first light—so what had happened to Jake Mullen, Charlie Piecemeal and Vince Claim? They backed off, lost heart, or had Quinton ...?

Rand swallowed on his dry, dusty throat. Suppose Quinton had got to them, slid out of these hills like some slow, silent rattler and taken them out one by one. Could be that even now he was watching the turn of events down there in the creek—and quietly cursing the woman for breaking out like she had. She had done nobody any favours, save maybe Luce Whitworth. He would not be slow to figure that the woman might prove useful.

But the real point was, would she tell as how she had been riding alongside Legget Rand? Or would she keep her mouth shut?

Rand swallowed again. What she said or did not say hardly mattered the bat of an eyelid right now. How to keep her alive was the priority. 'Damn her!' he muttered, and eased back, wincing at the throb of pain in his leg.

Nothing else for it, he reckoned, clearing more sweat, he would have to sit tight on Whitworth's tail and wait his chance. And meantime just hope that Quinton, wherever he was, kept his head and stayed calm. Any flying lead now might just go settling itself in the wrong body.

He turned to check that his mount was still hitched far side of the boulders and began to crawl out of the cover. He was figuring on Whitworth holding to the creek trail, not straying far; waiting for Quinton to show himself. But when and where would that be?

Rand winced again as the weaker leg dragged behind him like a log. One of these days he was going to get even with the fellow who had fired the wounding shot that night. Find him and take the greatest pleasure in—

Rand halted and lay flat on his stomach. There was a shadow moving close to him that had not been there before. A long, dark shadow that was sure as hell shaping up as if cast from somebody close. And that somebody could only be one man out here.

'Yuh were bitin' on dust last time I saw yuh, Mister Rand,' said the voice. 'Gettin' to make a habit of it, aren't yuh?'

THIRTEEN

She might look a scruffy, all-in wreck, thought Willard Hooper, but she was spitting fire faster than a she-devil. And she meant it. Anybody get to so much as thinking of laying a hand on her and she would bite it clean off. Jess Larson was not to be tampered with, not in this mood, but just precisely what they were going to do with her fooled him.

Did Whitworth know, he wondered?

'Yuh want me to rope her up?' asked Sharman, eyeing the woman carefully. 'Mebbe just her hands.'

'She ain't goin' no place,' said Whitworth. 'Don't look to have the strength.'

'I wouldn't bet on that,' drawled Hooper, lighting a cheroot and blowing a line of smoke. 'So what yuh have in mind now,

Luce? We goin' to peg the woman out like bait and wait for Quinton to come huntin'? Sounds a mite risky to me.'

'That we ain't goin' to do,' grinned Whitworth, 'fascinatin' though it might be. No, we push on, holdin' to this trail—all exceptin' Bob here, that is.'

'Yuh ain't expectin' me—' groaned Sharman.

'You, Bob, are goin' to get y'self up into them hills, real soft and silent like, slippin' about like a shadow, 'til we flush Quinton out. I wanna let him see the woman, but I wanna know where he is when he does, and I wanna know soon while the light's good and we got somethin' clear to shoot at. Yuh understand?'

'Sure,' said Sharman, 'but—'

'But nothin', Bob,' drawled Whitworth. 'It's all plain enough. Just get out there and do it. And no foulin' up. We got a real chance now of closin' the book on this little episode, so let's get to it, shall we?'

Hooper blew another curl of smoke.

Closing the book, he wondered, or simply turning a page?

'Been a while,' said Quinton, settling himself in the slim shade of the rocks and eyeing Legget Rand with a steady stare. 'Five whole years. Mangy for me, painful for you by the look of it. And now we're back where we started—down in the dirt.'

Rand wiped a lathering of sweat from his face. 'Not quite,' he croaked drily. 'Them sonsofbitches down there—'

'We'll get to them soon enough,' said Quinton softly. 'Let 'em sweat for an hour or so. Spook 'em up a mite. Pretty soon they're goin' to elect one of 'em to try flushin' me out.' He smiled. 'That'll be interestin', won't it? Meantime, Mister Rand, how come yuh out here, and why ain't yuh with the rest of them one-eyed scumbags?'

Rand relaxed. 'Guess yuh can figure that. Lost my badge in that mayhem five years back. Got m'self a crook leg, had no place to go, and ...' His eyes narrowed. 'I kinda reckoned there'd come a day when yuh'd be back, and I knew where I'd be standin' when yuh did. Benefice broke my life. I figure they owe me.'

'I'd reckon so,' grunted Quinton, 'but it's all real personal with me. I work alone. Do things my way.'

'Understood,' said Rand, 'but the fact is, Quinton, yuh ain't got a speck of a chance at the moment. Even if yuh get to takin' out Whitworth and Hooper, there's a whole town waitin' to see the last of yuh. More scared runnin' folk and guns than yuh could face. So mebbe—'

'Yuh mouthin' what sounds an awful lot like backin'-off talk, mister. Yuh here to persuade me against what I have in mind? That why yuh put y'self to all this trouble?'

'Well, mebbe yuh could think of—'

'Oh, no, Mister Rand, that I could not do. Not now. Not never. I been too long thinkin' on this day. That's been all my thinkin' for five years, and still is.' Quinton half-turned to gaze beyond the shade. 'Sorry to disappoint yuh, but that's the way of it.'

'Maybe we could get yuh a pardon,' said Rand quickly. 'Wipe the whole sorry mess clean off the record. Marshal Edgeworth is sure to go along with that once he sees how things stand. We could go get the woman, ride hard for Salton ... Three days at most and we could have things straightened, cleared up, with y'self still alive and standin'.'

'And you, mister,' asked Quinton, 'what about you?'

'If I can get to livin' without that lynchin' rattlin' round my sleep—'

'Then go do it, Rand,' snapped Quinton, turning sharply, his Colt tight and steady in his hand. 'Go do it—your way, any way yuh choose, and leave me to mine.'

'Yuh makin' one helluva mistake,' murmured Rand. 'Yuh know that, don't yuh?'

'Sure, just like I did the day I rode into Benefice.'

Rand cleared more sweat from his face. 'What about Jess Larson?' he croaked. 'She figure any place in *your* way?'

'Not right now she don't,' said Quinton. 'No place at all.'

Thick-headed mule, thought Rand, pausing to catch his breath in the slow crawl back to his mount, about as straight thinking as a hen bird nesting pine cones. Blinkered, obsessed; no reasoning with the fellow—but, then, was that so surprising? Had he really reckoned on walking up to Quinton and leading him back to Salton calm as a wet calf? Hell, no!

But now what?

Forget Quinton for sure, at least until there came a chance to get Jess Larson out of Whitworth's hands. Then—well, then he might just get back to sitting tight in Quinton's shadow. If the fellow was intent on riding into Benefice—and he surely was—somebody had to be watching his back. What happened up front would come soon enough.

Rand crawled on. How long, he wondered, before Whitworth sent Sharman —almost certainly Sharman—to flush Quinton out? And how long then for Sharman against Quinton's gun? But, meantime, the woman ...

Rand licked angrily at the sweat and dirt. He had to get to her somehow, maybe soon as Sharman was in the hills. Thing was, he pondered, to stay wide awake, get himself some place where he could watch, well hidden, out of sight of all eyes but close enough to see exactly what was happening, wherever it happened. He winced at the stab of pain in his leg, paused a moment, listened and moved on.

'Stay awake,' he murmured to himself. 'Just stay awake, yuh lame old fool!'

But Legget Rand's eyes were already closed long before he reached his mount.

FOURTEEN

Bob Sharman could feel his fear, like cold hands knotting his guts, oozing through the sweat that dripped from his chin, in the ache of tired legs as he scrambled ever higher into the hills. This was some fool-headed effort, sure enough, he thought, reaching for the next hold among the hot rocks, with about as much chance of succeeding as he had of shooting holes through the moon.

Damnit, it was typical of Luce Whitworth—always find somebody else to dip his hands in the dirt. That was the way of things with Luce, always had been save when the odds were all stacked with him. Take that night of the lynching: Luce had been there with the rest of them, right at the heart of it all, but he had sure as hell not fired them shots into Legget Rand until he was certain the sheriff was standing alone. Not Luce, nossir. His own skin was always stretched tighter than the next fellow's.

And who had been first in line to take Rand's badge? Luce Whitworth. Who had accused Quinton? Luce Whitworth. And who had Willard Hooper tight in his pocket to ensure the best of town living? Just guess!

Even so, Quinton's return had rattled him some and Vince Claim's death in that manner had done nothing to settle his nerves. But that had been no excuse for what happened to Jake and Charlie. Luce would get to paying for that one day. You bet he would.

And now he had the woman. She spelled trouble. A woman always did when you got to using her. Hell, what guarantee was there anyhow that Quinton gave a cuss for Jess Larson? Quinton had only one thing in mind and he was staying with it, woman or no woman. So chances were that all this, scuffing around in the dirt of these hills, was one heap of a waste of time. Quinton was probably holed-up some place taking it easy, just preparing himself for the ride into Benefice. He could take Whitworth any time it suited.

Or anybody else, come to that.

Sharman halted between rock shelves and wiped the sweat from his face. One thing was for sure, he reckoned, gazing over the heat-shimmered dirt, scrub and stone, Quinton was in no hurry to show himself. And, damnit, he could be anywhere. Any one of the clefts over there; those shadowed places between boulders; or maybe lurking in the cooler shade of that pine outcrop top of the ridge.

Now there was a thought. Sensible fellow would rest up in shade, stay cool, keep his mount easy and fly-free. Obvious. If Quinton was anywhere, he was up there in the pines. But getting to him unseen was not going to be that simple.

Sharman grunted. Maybe the answer was to work a way to the rear of the pines. If Quinton was keeping any sort of watch, he would be concentrating on the slope to the creek. Could be he was unaware of anybody up here, reckoning on being alone with all the time in the world to make his move whenever he chose. Could be he was in for a surprise.

Or somebody was.

Sharman moved again, this time at a faster pace to the boulders. Once there, he figured, he could work out the safest way to the back of the pines, some track through the shadows, and then, if he got lucky, he could flush Quinton into the clear and down the slope. It would be up to Whitworth and Hooper from there on. Not that Hooper would be a deal of use. No, this was going to be Luce Whitworth's show to the very last spit of lead.

Whoever caught it.

Sharman reached the boulders in a lather of swimming sweat, fell into the shade between them, and heaved a long, deep breath. Hell, it was hot, too darned hot for scuttling about like a turkey round the cooking pot. He could do with a beer—two beers—and the fussing of one of them fancy Hooper girls. Maybe that one with the short black hair and the big brown eyes ...

He stiffened at the sound of a trembling fall of pebbles, narrowed his gaze on the pine stand high above him and did not move. There was somebody hereabouts, sure enough, somebody shifting his feet, setting them pebbles loose, maybe coming this way. But did he know what he was coming to, or had he already seen it?

Sharman swallowed and settled himself on his haunches. Time had come for silence, not a movement, not so much as a blink. Just wait and listen.

No more tumbling pebbles. Nothing of anything. So had the fellow—Quinton, for sure—halted? Was he watching? How long would he wait? What the hell was he waiting for, anyhow? Playing rattler stalking lizard like this could go on for hours, wear a fellow down, spook him up to thinking the sound of his own breath was somebody else's. Hell, this was no time for getting twitchy.

Nor did he, for in the next moment Bob Sharman was standing upright, stiff and straight as the pine trunks above him, the goose bumps on his shoulders wet with fresh sweat at the sound of the click of the Colt at his back.

'No movin', fella, not if yuh want to stay breathin' a mite longer,' said the voice quietly. 'Now just do as I say and you and me'll get along just fine. Take it easy. Drop that gunbelt. Relax, then slip yuh feet real slow out of them nice-lookin' boots of yours.'

Bob Sharman did precisely as he was told without once looking round to see just who it was giving the orders.

'Good,' said the voice again. 'Yuh did that real well. Now for the socks, and then yuh shirt. Keepin' it easy, fella, slow and easy.'

'What the hell's this all about, mister?' croaked Sharman, reaching for his socks.

'Well, now,' came the voice again, 'I'll tell yuh while yuh strippin' down there. I guess yuh know who I am—name's Quinton—and I sure know your face well enough, fella. One of the Benefice mob, eh? Right? Right—and I also know just why yuh here and what yuh were plannin'. Sorry, but it ain't going to work on account of how yuh goin' for a walk, a long, hot walk from which I doubt if yuh'll return. Yuh hearin' me, fella?'

'Sure,' said Sharman, slipping out of his shirt. 'But—'

'Now this walk is goin' to take yuh out of these hills clear to the start of the desert, and that's where I'm goin' to leave yuh, leastways once I'm sure yuh headin' straight. It'll be hot, then freezin' cold, and you with no water, no boots, no shirt, no hat, most of nothin' save yuh pants. 'Course, yuh'll try turnin' back, but by then them feet of yours'll be sore as fire, all blistered up and bleedin', and it's sure goin' to take one hell of an effort to put one foot in front of the other. I know, I've been there, fella. No knowin' what'll happen to yuh, or what sorta state yuh'll be in when somebody finally finds yuh, if anybody ever does, but I ain't one bit bothered.

'There now, I'm all through. Let's get started, shall we? We got some ways to go and I'm in a hurry, so step it out, fella, step it out ...'

'He ain't comin' back, Luce, I can smell he ain't. He's gone, and I sure as hell know who's shot him.' Willard Hooper paused at the end of his measured pacing, gazed into the already night-shadowed hills, then turned to face Luce Whitworth where he sat twisting a length of rope through his fingers. 'Been hours since he left,' he added drily.

'I know how long it's been,' said Whitworth, knotting the rope tightly.

'So we ready to pull out now? Call it a day like we should've done a day back?' He crossed to the deeper shadow where Jess Larson sat with her back to a rock. 'And what we goin' to do about her? We leave her, or she comin' with us?'

Whitworth tugged at the knot then spat noisily into the dirt. 'Assumin' a lot, ain't yuh, Hooper?' he drawled through a cold glare. 'Assumin' Quinton's gotten to Bob; assumin' we're pullin' out; assumin' the woman figures. What's with yuh, f'Crissake? Lost yuh stomach for what we all agreed to do?'

'There's yuh problem, Luce,' said Hooper, moving closer, 'we just ain't done what we set out to do. Nothin' like it. And now it's down to the two of us, with not a spit on the wind's chance of pullin' this off. Only one thing to do as I see it: get outa this godforsaken land and back to town. We wait for Quinton there—with guns at our side. Makes sense—the only sense. Yuh agree?'

'And if I don't?' scowled Whitworth.

'Yuh will if yuh wanna go on wearin' that badge.'

Whitworth's glare darkened for a moment then eased as he dropped the knotted rope. 'Have it your way,' he said, coming to his feet. 'But the woman comes with us. I ain't leavin' her for Quinton to hear what we doin'. We'll settle with her when the time comes.'

'Whatever yuh like, I ain't fussed. All I want is out, fast as we can. We ride through the night, should make town by noon. Let's move.'

Neither Willard Hooper nor Luce Whitworth saw the soft smile at Jess Larson's lips, nor could they have read her thoughts as she pondered on the day when Quinton would ride into Benefice.

And that, she reckoned, was not to be missed.

FIFTEEN

There was a chill edge to the early night air when Legget Rand twitched out of sleep and shivered to his feet. 'Hell!' he cursed, blinking rapidly, slapping his arms across his chest, then rubbing his eyes until they were focused on the gloom. He was getting too old for this sort of caper; too old, too worn, too darned set in his ways. Fellow could have got himself killed sleeping like that!

He rubbed vigorously at his lame leg as he peered over the stretch of hills and listened to the silence. Quiet as the grave, he thought, but just who had claimed one in the last few hours? Where was Quinton; still out here somewhere, or had he moved on? And what of Jess Larson—was she still with Whitworth, still alive?

He grunted. No good would come of standing about. Time to round up his mount, take a closer look at the creek down there, whatever he might find, and try figuring just what Quinton was planning now. More to the point, where he was.

But it was a long hour later before Rand finally concluded that he was alone in the hills; that Quinton was not close and that Whitworth had called off the hunt and doubtless high-tailed it back to Benefice, taking the woman with him.

So now, he reckoned, he had a simple choice. He could either take to the trail and be right there in town when Quinton rode in, or he could play one last wild card and try once again to join up with Quinton before he headed for his showdown.

Damn it, if the fellow thought he was going to ride into Benefice and stay alive long enough to settle his scores in his time, he was plumb crazy. Whitworth and Hooper would have more guns ranged against him than he would ever get to counting. If he made it ten steps into the main street he could have gotten lucky.

But with somebody at his side, who knew every plank and nail of the town, every nook and cranny, where to be, where not to be, and where Whitworth would position his guns—well, that might, just might, give Quinton some sort of chance. Slim and short-lived, maybe, but a chance. That much he had earned for those five years in Jamesville. All the rest, he figured, would be history.

Legget Rand picked up the main trail for Benefice a half-hour later, firm in his resolve to stay with it through the dark and until he was within a mile or so of town. Then he would wait. Quinton would be there sooner or later, and not for him, he reckoned, some skulking backdoor arrival. No, he would ride up clear as a rock mound in a desert, probably in the dusty haze of dawn, the gathering light behind him, hands easy on the reins, his gaze steady, tight and fixed on only one thing—the town that had brought down the curtain on the longest nights of his life.

Shadowing that same trail at the time that Rand reached it was Frank Quinton, riding slow and gentle, in no hurry, holding to the darker depths of the silent land and reckoning he could keep this up for as long as that fool rider out there kept going.

Say this for the fellow though, he was thinking, he was persistent. He could have ridden anywhere, cleared the territory, holed-up some place over the border, stayed in the hills until all this was finished.

But not Legget Rand.

Rand was a scarred man, and bitter with it; stubborn, too, judging by the way he was sitting that horse out there. Straight as a ramrod, eyes tight on the way ahead, no concern for the night. And there was no problem figuring his thinking. He was planning on being there when Quinton rode into Benefice. One last attempt to try dissuading him against settling the scores, or did Rand have something else in mind—like standing to Quinton's side when the lead began to fly?

Darn fool if that was on his mind! No good reason for Rand to go getting himself any deeper into this, maybe killed for a fellow he hardly knew. No man went to his Boot Hill for as slim a cause as that. Not, that is, unless he was Legget Rand—or, come to that, as bone-headed set on his destiny as Frank Quinton. Hell, they were alike as two eggs on the same plate!

Well, there was maybe something could be done about that, thought Quinton, reining deeper into the darkness. He would just have to stay with Rand until sun-up, keep him in sight, then settle the issue once and for all long before they reached Benefice.

Meantime, he went back to thinking about Jess Larson and wondering if he would get to seeing her again. That was another issue to be settled.

There was just one big issue on Luce Whitworth's mind as he rode hard behind Jess Larson and Willard Hooper—when and where to rein up, pull clear of the trail and go hide himself in the rocks to await Quinton's arrival. Hooper would not agree, his only thought was of Benefice and getting himself back to his saloon, but Whitworth was not planning on giving him a choice. If it was possible to stop Quinton now, then somebody had to make the move. Once the fellow hit town all hell would erupt, with no telling the outcome or who might still be standing to see it.

Stop Quinton any way, at any price, was still the itch in the palm of Whitworth's gun hand. And this might be the last chance he would have.

'Hold it there!' he yelled above the thud of hoofs, at the same time reining hard against his mount's snorting prance. He waited until Hooper and the woman had halted and were sitting their horses easy before approaching.

'What now?' snapped Hooper irritably. 'We ain't got no time for restin' up.'

'Ain't plannin' on restin' up,' said Whitworth. 'I'm plannin' on leavin' yuh right here. Yuh go on to town alone.'

'And just what the hell fool thinkin' is that?' snapped Hooper again.

'Simple enough,' grinned Whitworth. 'Yuh don't want Quinton in town any more than I do. Yuh want it over, soon as yuh can, so that's what I'm deliverin'.'

'How?' said Hooper, his eyes narrowing. 'Yuh tried stoppin' him once and lost four good men for the trouble. What's different now? Situation ain't changed none, way I see it.'

'Well, that ain't so surprisin', Willard, seein' as how yuh *seein'* seems to get a mite blinkered these days. But I'll overlook that.' Whitworth's grin flashed to a smile, then faded. 'I figure on Quinton bein' an hour, no more than two, behind us.

He should be passin' through here just before it's full light—and I'll be waitin', somewhere up there in them rocks. One shot from that Winchester of yours will end it, so hand over the piece and ride on. Yuh'll be seein' me soon after noon.'

Hooper sighed, grunted, drew the rifle from its scabbard and tossed it to Whitworth. 'Suit y'self. I ain't arguin'; you're the one makin' the choice. Just hope yuh right this time.'

'Yuh'll be chewin' on yuh words when yuh pourin' me that drink later,' grinned Whitworth. 'Now shift yuh butts outa here and keep goin'. And don't let that woman stray none. I ain't done with her yet.'

Whitworth watched Hooper and the woman rein about to the main trail and ride on, then settled the Winchester across his lap and eased his mount softly into the scattering of loose rocks that bordered the higher cover on the bluff. First light was still some time away, but when the slow drift of it reached out of that eastern sky,

Quinton would be there, a lone rider on a silent, dawn-pebbled trail.

And all the rest, he reckoned, would be easy.

SIXTEEN

Morning air, fresh as clear water over smooth, cold rocks, and a soft breeze back of it. Fellow could hardly ask for more after a long night ride, thought Legget Rand, easing on the reins to bring his mount to a walk through the growing light. Time now to call a halt, find himself some cover, rest the horse and wait.

And maybe for not so long at that, he reckoned, if Quinton had kept moving through the dark. You bet—oh, yes, you bet, mused Rand, kept moving and no looking back. He would be here soon enough. Meantime, Whitworth and whoever was riding with him would be closing fast on Benefice. How had they treated Jess Larson, he wondered? Maybe just dragged her along for now, but once in town, once the liquor was flowing ... She would be the first to get to when the dust had settled. Always assuming ...

Hell, there he went again, thinking wrong side of the fence before he had reached it. Been too long in the saddle, too long for that darned leg, too long to hold his thinking straight. Most certainly time for that rest before he got to seeing things.

But Legget Rand saw nothing in the next few seconds. Nothing of the shape that rose from the rocks on the bluff to his left, nothing of the barrel that targeted on him as he drifted like a blur through the pale morning light, nothing of the man's steady hands, the gleam in his eyes.

All that crossed his line of vision then was the sudden rearing head of the mount beneath him and a creasing of the light that seemed unreal, as if the day had given up already and let the night move back. And all he felt was pain burning deep and fiery into him.

And then he saw and felt nothing.

He would live, but it was going to be a close-run thing, thought Quinton watching the man carefully. The shot had buried its lead deep in the fleshy quarter of Rand's chest; another fingernail lower and it would have been the long sleep for the one-time sheriff. Even so, that bleeding ... Quinton grunted. Fellow needed a doc, he grunted again. No doubt about who the sonofabitch behind the rifle had thought he had in his sights: dark shape of a tired, lone rider who had been in the saddle most of the night, dead set on the trail for Benefice; had to be Quinton.

Gunman must have been really convinced he had got his man; never bothered to check; just high-tailed it out of the rocks and disappeared. Too bad he had not taken that closer look, but maybe an oversight Quinton could use to his advantage come the time. But that would have to wait. Priority right now was that doc.

'Yuh hearin' me, Rand?' said Quinton squatting closer. 'Don't try speakin'. Just indicate yuh understand what I'm sayin'.' Rand croaked a faint murmur as his eyes strained to open. 'It's me, Quinton. Been trailin' yuh most of the night. Should've gotten closer by the look of it. But that's as mebbe. Fact is yuh hit bad and there ain't a deal I can do about it. Yuh need a doc.'

Rand croaked again through a trickle of blood at the corner of his mouth.

'Easy, fella, easy,' soothed Quinton. 'Now listen. Can't risk movin' yuh to your mount. Yuh'd never make it. So I'm going' to make the best of things for yuh right here, then go fetch the doc out of Benefice. That fella Raynes, ain't it?' Rand murmured and swallowed. 'Right, so I'll get him and send him out to yuh. Yuh got that? Good. Meantime, yuh just don't move, understand? Stay real quiet and leave the rest to me—which is what yuh should've done all along, damn yuh!'

Quinton smiled and laid a hand on Rand's shoulder. 'Appreciate yuh good intentions, though. Would've done the same m'self.'

Rand's mouth opened. 'Whit— Whit—' he hissed.

'Yeah, I got it. Whitworth,' said Quinton. 'He must've held back here waitin' for me. Pity he missed out, but I got that pleasure to come.'

Rand groaned again as his eyes closed. Just no stopping the mule-headed fellow, he thought, through a surge of pain. Just no stopping him.

Jess Larson turned from the window of the room above Hooper's Saloon, crossed to the locked door and rattled the knob defiantly. A pointless gesture, she thought, tightening her lips, but at least it let everybody know her spirit had not broken. If Willard Hooper thought for one minute ...

'Hell!' she snapped to herself, turning again and folding her arms angrily across her breasts. 'Hell!' She stood stiff and erect for a moment, then relaxed. No point in wasting time and energy fuming and spitting, that was going nowhere fast. She had to think, do something, get to planning where she was going to figure in all this when Quinton rode in—*if* Quinton rode in.

Supposing that scumbag Luce Whitworth had succeeded? Supposing he had taken Quinton by surprise? But had anybody ever taken Quinton by surprise? Somebody sure as hell had five years back. The whole darned town, day they had handed him over to that marshal! That had been some surprise and no mistake. Still, that was five years back. Things were different now. Quinton was different, and he *was* the difference. Even so, there were more guns ranged against him here than any man could hope to face and stay alive for longer than it took for fingers to ease back on triggers. No balancing the odds in a situation like that, not unless Legget Rand had a card up his sleeve. Not unless ...

Not unless the 'aces' were out of the pack. Supposing Hooper was not around come the showdown? Supposing Quinton had got to Whitworth first—that would leave only Hooper to prime the town guns, and maybe without him there might not be such a readiness to face the angry man out of Jamesville. Folk always needed a spark before they got to thinking of fire. No spark, no fire.

Jess Larson was smiling softly to herself when she reached the window again and stood watching the gathering day's heat begin to shimmer over the dirt street below her. She had the makings of a plan that might just work if the luck was sitting right there on her shoulder.

But seconds later the smile had faded, the plan numbed in her thought as if kicked by a bucking stallion at the sight of Luce Whitworth riding hell-bent into town with a look of triumph on his face.

'Hell!' she snapped, and stomped back to the door.

Doc Raynes stayed where he was in the shaded stretch of the boardwalk and watched Luce Whitworth rein his mount to a slithering, dust-clouded halt at Hooper's Saloon.

Trouble, he thought, slipping his hands into the pockets of his frock coat, big trouble. Whitworth's arrival could mean only one thing—that he had taken Quinton by surprise out there on the trail. Hooper had reckoned he would never pull it off. Hooper had been wrong, and that would put Whitworth right where he wanted to be—top of the stinking pile.

Trouble, and not a man here who would raise so much as a spit to douse it. Who would even dare to. Whitworth would have Benefice tight in his grip by nightfall.

Doc Raynes sighed and walked slowly,

thoughtfully towards his home at the far end of the street. At least there might be some peace there, he reckoned—for a while.

SEVENTEEN

It was mid-afternoon on that same day when Doc Raynes realized it was no pesky fly disturbing his doze in the airless back room. No buzz for one thing, and no fly hatched made the floorboards creak, big as they were in these parts. No, this was no fly he had for company, unless he was dreaming, and that he was not.

This, he figured, was a visitor of the two-legged kind.

Even so, Doc Raynes stayed where he was slumped in the folds of the vast armchair, his eyes closed, beads of sweat standing proud on his brow, a trickle of it slipping down his cheek to the crevice of his collar. Whoever the visitor was he was keen to stay quiet, in no hurry to announce himself, maybe just standing there in the

163

shadowed half of the room waiting his chance to come closer.

Closer for what, wondered Doc? Seemed a silent, creeping visitor at this hour could have only one thing in mind, but he was sure as hell taking his time about it! So maybe now was the time to make a fast move for that Colt there in the drawer of his desk. Would he make it? No chance. The desk was too far away and the drawer locked. It would take a whole minute to go find the key.

Doc shifted as if twitching in his sleep, licked at his lips and tried his darndest to keep his eyelids from fluttering. That was always the giveaway when feigning sleep; the eyelids were the nerve ends straining like tied drapes to swish open to the light. Sooner or later they won, and sooner was going to be right now ...

Doc Raynes' eyes snapped open in the same moment his visitor spoke.

'Thought for a minute there yuh were

out for the count,' murmured Quinton, stepping from the shadows. 'Yuh all through sleepin'?'

'Sure,' muttered Doc, struggling to a sitting position, wiping a hand over his sticky face. 'I wasn't expectin'—'

'Visitors,' said Quinton, 'least of all me. Yuh remember?'

'Yuh bet I do. Only too well. But what—'

'Ain't the occasion for a deal of talkin', Doc. It's taken too long for me to get this far, and time's runnin' out. I got a job for yuh, real urgent, and I want yuh saddled up and out of town faster than it's takin' the tellin'.' Quinton glanced quickly at the window. 'Town's quiet right now, so I figure yuh can slip away without bein' noticed. Yuh reckon?'

'Sure—if I knew where I was goin' and for why.'

Quinton grunted. 'It's Rand, hurt bad, out there on the trail. Took a shot from Whitworth meant for me. Lucky he ain't a stiff. Nothin' much I can do for him. He needs a doc.'

Raynes heaved himself to his feet, crossed to his desk and began packing his bag. 'Yuh trustin' me to slip away?' he murmured, his back to Quinton. 'I could just as easy go raise Whitworth and the town.' He turned sharply. 'They're waitin' on yuh, Quinton. Yuh ain't got a deal of the odds stacked your way.'

Quinton grunted again. 'I'm trustin' yuh, Doc, 'cus I figure fixin' Legget Rand is more your line of decency than seein' me eatin' dirt. Second, Rand tried helpin' me see the sense of not comin' back here. I owe him for that. As for them odds yuh speak of, yuh can leave them to me.'

Doc Raynes concentrated on his black bag. 'Whitworth's back and it's my bet he's fixin' on makin' this town his own, specially now he figures he's taken care of you. Boastin' of it back there at the saloon, yuh can bet.' Doc turned again. 'He'll be the hero, Quinton, with the town at his feet. How the hell yuh goin'—'

'Hooper have a woman with him when he rode in?' snapped Quinton.

'Jess Larson. Got her locked away some place. But she ain't—'

'Just finish messin' with that bag, Doc, and get y'self outa here. I'll see yuh later.'

'Sure yuh will,' sighed Raynes, 'but I don't reckon we'll be finishin' this conversation. You'll be dead, Quinton, sure as I'm standin' here. But I'll clean yuh up best I can for your coffin.'

'Much obliged,' grunted out Quinton. 'Now, f'Crissake, go do yuh best for Rand. I'll see yuh in hell if yuh don't.'

Doc Raynes slipped into his jacket, settled his hat on his head, and reached for his bag. 'Knew it'd come to this,' he croaked, facing Quinton. 'Tried to say as much, but nobody was listenin'.'

'Nobody ever is, Doc, 'til what yuh tryin' to say gets to hauntin'. Then they are. Hearin' yuh loud and clear.'

Willard Hooper slid another bottle of his best whiskey across the table to Luce Whitworth and leaned back in his chair, his gaze dark and narrowed on the smiling, sweat-streaked face of the young sheriff. Another half-hour of this and he would be all for putting a bullet clean between those blue boasting eyes.

'Tell it again, Luce,' came a voice from the back of the crowded, smoke-filled saloon. 'As it was.'

'And no missin' the details, Luce,' echoed another.

'Tell how the sonofabitch went down, Luce.'

'How many shots, Luce?'

'Yuh get him with the first?'

'How'd he look when he knew? He get the shakes, Luce?'

'Never knew a thing, eh? Just went down.'

'Swatted like a fly!'

'Come on, Luce, one more time, eh?'

Whitworth took a long gulp from the fresh bottle and wiped a hand across his mouth. 'OK, hold it there, fellas,' he drawled. 'One more time on account of how I know yuh all wanna relish the fact that Quinton ain't no more—and another thing, to the memory of them good fellas who rode right alongside of me and sadly lost their lives in the service of our town here.'

'S'right, Luce,' called a man at the bar. 'To them—Charlie, Jake and the others.'

Whitworth staggered to his feet. 'So here's how it was just them few hours back, m'self alone up there in them rocks ...'

Hooper sighed and blew a thick cloud of smoke from his cigar. Lying scumbag, he thought, his stare tight on Whitworth's face. And a dangerous liar at that. Give the fellow half a chance and he would be holding this town in a grip nobody would break. Taking over, that was his thinking—sheriff's badge, town store, livery, whatever took his fancy, saloon included, and the girls. The hell he would! Trouble was, how to stop him when he had the mob with him? If Rand had been here ...

Just where *had* Legget Rand buried himself? He gone into hiding, ridden out? Not Rand. Lame oldster had no place to go. But he had to be some place.

Hooper blew more smoke. Rand, Whitworth, Jess Larson—a nest of hornets between them. Whole situation needed sorting out, fast, while there was still time.

'How come yuh didn't bring Quinton's body in, Luce?' drawled a man at the bar. 'Would've been somethin' to see him. So why didn't yuh?'

'Yeah, why didn't yuh?' agreed a drunk at the man's side.

The bar filled with soft murmurings, and then a long silence as all eyes went back to the sheriff. Whitworth leaned heavily on the table for a moment, let his stare sweep over the faces in front of him, then came fully upright again, stiff and straight. 'Weren't the time,' he snapped. 'Needed to get back here, didn't I?'

'Time it takes to load a body wouldn't have made a deal of difference,' said the man at the bar.

Whitworth's stare darkened. 'So what yuh sayin', fella?' he asked.

'Ain't sayin' nothin', Luce, 'cepting as how it would've been somethin' to see the sonofabitch.'

'Yeah,' spluttered the drunk, ' 'course it would. Anyhow, how'd yuh know it was Quinton yuh shot? How do *we* know?' He reeled and reached to a table for support. 'How about that, Sheriff? I ain't seen no body, not a hide nor hair of one. Last time I saw Quinton he was alive. I sure ain't seen him *dead*. Have you?'

The bar fell silent again, all eyes concentrated on Whitworth. Hooper shifted in his chair, crossed his legs, and blew a long, thin line of smoke.

A fine sheeting of sweat gleamed on the sheriff's face as he eased his weight to one foot and began to smile. ' 'Course I have,' he said through a half laugh. 'Saw him drop from his horse like a stone. That shot of mine—'

'Yuh shot *somebody*,' slurred the drunk, 'but was it Quinton?'

Whitworth's smile faded slowly, disappearing from his lips as if blown away on some chilling breeze to be replaced by a darkening scowl. 'I don't like the tone of what yuh sayin', old-timer,' he said. 'Fact, from how I'm hearin' it, I'd say yuh callin' me a liar.'

The drunk reeled again, his hands thudding flat on the table. 'And mebbe yuh are at that, Luce Whitworth.'

A man not caught up in the tension of that moment might have counted out the seconds it took for the scowl on Whitworth's face to deepen to a thunderous black, for his right hand to flash to his Colt, draw it, and for the roar of the single shot to fill the bar with the sound of a hell exploding.

But nobody was counting. Nobody was moving save to shift their eyes to the drunk, see the blood begin to soak through his vest, his gaze glisten and then settle to a dull blindness, his body to twitch once, twice, before sliding to the floor, dragging the table with it.

There were gasps, groans. Somebody dropped a glass. Some fellow set teeth on edge with the scrape of his chair as he jumped to his feet. A bar girl stifled a scream, another began to cry. But it was Willard Hooper who was the first to move, coming upright at Whitworth's side with a speed that had the barrel of his gun tight in the sheriff's side before he could take breath.

'Weren't no need for that, Luce,' said Hooper slowly, his cigar rolling in the corner of his mouth. 'Old soak didn't

mean yuh no harm. Wasn't even carryin'
a sidepiece.' He paused. 'That's murder,
Luce. And murder's a hangin' offence
hereabouts.'

EIGHTEEN

It was mention of the word 'hanging' that changed the mood in Hooper's Saloon. It hung there for a moment in the echo of the measured tone of Hooper's voice, then seemed like the smoke to settle, missing no one, getting deeper into them as if being inhaled, until somebody, the voice of everyone, murmured: 'He's right. That's murder. That's a hangin'.'

Whitworth dropped his Colt to the table and gestured wildly. 'What the hell yuh talkin' about?' he croaked. 'Ain't I just been out there puttin' an end to Quinton for the good of all of yuh, so's yuh can all sleep easy in yuh beds? What sorta goddamn gratitude yuh handin' out, f'Crissake? Ain't I done enough?'

'More than enough,' snapped Hooper,

seizing the moment before another voice was raised. ' 'Cus what yuh ain't done is get to the tellin' of what really happened to Charlie Piecemeal and Jake Mullen out there, how yuh killed the pair of 'em, and how yuh sure as hell sent Bob Sharman to his certain death. That's enough, ain't it? I'd reckon so.'

The crowded bar began to stir. 'And we still don't know for sure that Quinton's dead,' came a lone voice. 'We ain't seen a body.'

'And now this,' came another. 'The old fella here, shot down like a dog.'

'Yuh do all as Hooper says?' growled a man. 'He tellin' the truth, Luce?'

'Yuh get to believin' him—' began Whitworth.

'I do,' drawled a lean man stepping forward. 'Willard ain't got no cause to lie, not that I can see. Why should he? Stands to lose as much as anyone. And what about Quinton? I ain't settlin' to him bein' dead 'til I seen a body—but I sure seen what happened here and that's a hangin'. We done it once, we can do it again!'

The gathering murmured, talked louder, took up the word 'hanging' as if in a chant. Whitworth sweated, Hooper grinned, then held up a hand and shouted for silence.

'All right, boys, all right,' he called. 'Seems like we got a unanimous verdict here, but we gotta think careful before we get to actin'. We gotta get back to figurin' on Quinton, 'cus if he ain't dead he's certain-sure headin' this way, so I reckon on us playin' Whitworth as a real ace.'

'What's yuh thinkin', Willard?' asked the lean man.

'We hold our sheriff right here in one of his own cells 'til Quinton rides in. I figure that'll be sun-up t'morrow. Then we bargain Whitworth for him ridin' on. My bettin' is Quinton'll settle for the score bein' even once he's dealt with Luce.'

'And if Quinton don't ride in?' said the man.

'We get to a hangin', anyhow,' smiled Hooper. 'Same time—sun-up.'

'I'll see yuh in hell!' mouthed Whitworth.

'Yuh will, Luce,' drawled Hooper. 'Yuh surely will.'

Jess Larson heard the key turn in the lock and knew instinctively who would be there when the door opened. She had heard the shot, the shouting in the bar below, and seen Luce Whitworth bundled away in the direction of the jail. God alone knew what was happening, she had thought, but whatever it was, however events were turning, it seemed certain that Willard Hooper had somehow taken charge.

Well, now,' said Hooper, stepping into the room, closing the door behind him, 'yuh all rested up, ma'am, takin' it easy?'

'No, I ain't!' flared Jess instantly, turning from the window. 'And no intention of doin' so.'

'Pity,' said Hooper through a lingering grin. 'I was kinda hopin'—'

'Go on hopin', mister, it's as close as yuh get!'

'Mebbe, but not yet awhiles, leastways 'til yuh all cleaned up some. Yuh in sore need of a bath, ma'am, and no mistake!'

Jess began to flare again, paused a moment, her gaze suddenly steady and narrowed, and folded her arms. 'What yuh have in mind?' she asked.

'Decent bathhouse 'cross the street at Charlie Piecemeal's old place,' smiled Hooper. 'No charge either, seein' as how Charlie ain't around no more. Could fix yuh up there.'

Jess held her stare into Hooper's hungry eyes. 'That so?' she murmured, unfolding her arms. 'Well, I might just take yuh up on that, mister, seein' as how that trail dirt eats into yuh, 'specially when a woman's bein' cooped up like a chicken.'

Hooper grunted. 'I'll get somebody take yuh across, keep an eye on yuh.'

'One eye'll be enough if he's got any sense!' snapped Jess as Hooper left the

179

room, missing the brightening twinkle in the woman's eyes.

Twenty minutes later, Jess Larson had been marched from the saloon to the deserted barber's shop under the leering, watchful eye of one of Hooper's sidekicks, a bull-shouldered, lumbering fellow by the name of Zac, whose only claim to being noticed was his size and his deeply scarred left cheek.

'Don't get no ideas, fella, while I'm in there,' said Jess at the door to the bathhouse. 'Yuh so much as breathe too close and I'll have half the town scuttling over here. Understand?'

The man had grunted, smiled, licked his lips and finally settled himself to wait in the barber's chair.

No hot water, but water, cold and fresh and soothing, for all that, thought Jess, slipping out of her dirt-stained clothes once satisfied that the stool propped under the knob of the door would hold long enough when the sidekick's curiosity got the better of him—as it would! Water and time ...

It was the time she valued more than the chance to clean up. Just how long had she got, she wondered, to make the most of being out of range of Hooper's eye? How long would it take for the sidekick's sweating lust to reach boiling point? Ten minutes, fifteen? She would keep the washing to a minimum, make it fast but sound as if she was relishing it.

She glanced anxiously round the room—door, tub, water butt, pails, stool, low table. Not a deal else, but there was a window, small and high, that looked out, she guessed, on the rear of the building. She could reach it, sure enough, maybe squeeze through it at a pinch, but, hell, she was going to need some luck once through, or worse, once halfway through. Somebody was certain to see her. And that would be goodbye freedom and a shivering welcome to trouble, Hooper-style.

But it was worth taking the chance. It was all she had going for her right now.

Town seemed peaceful enough, she thought, most of the menfolk being gathered in the saloon discussing whatever scheming plot Hooper had hatched. Maybe they would stay there. Maybe she would have a clear run. Clear run to where? It was one thing to be free, something else to know what to do with the freedom. Quinton would know all about that. And just where was he and what had happened to Legget Rand?

She closed her eyes on the maze of her thinking and splashed the cool water over her face and naked body. It felt good, almost too good to rush, but the minutes were pressing, time running out. That sidekick's thick head would be filling with pictures he could hardly resist and just about ready to push his luck as far as it would reach. What the hell! One last splash of that water ...

And then she knew the man was out of his chair and at the door.

She could hear him shuffling at the

threshold, hear his breathing, darned near feel the tension raging in him. Dare he, should he, had he the guts to burst through the door, take what he wanted, gamble his luck against Hooper's anger? The decision was getting awful close and there was no time now, thought Jess, to make it to the window, let alone get through it.

She was struggling with her clothes, heaving and scrambling against the cling of them against her wet body, when she heard the tap on the door.

Tap? What sort of a scumbag sidekick was it that went about tapping an announcement when he was all goosed up with lust? Did he expect her to open the door and welcome him with a willing smile?

The sweat on Jess Larson's face dripped to hcr breasts as she edged closer to the door. Another tap, a touch louder this time. Silence. Then the voice: 'Get y'self dressed and out here—fast.'

Quinton!

His hand was across her mouth, his grip tightening her body to him almost before she was out of the room.

'Don't say nothin', don't do nothin' save what I tell yuh,' hissed Quinton, guiding her across the barber's shop to the back door. Jess glanced quickly at the sidekick slumped in the chair, a deep, dark bloodstain spreading over his chest.

'What happened to him?' she whispered.

'Careless shaver. Cut his own throat,' murmured Quinton, opening the door to the shadowed back alley.

NINETEEN

Dust on brushed velvet annoyed him, made him feel uncomfortable, fidgety, like he was losing his grip—or was it a show of jangled nerves?

Willard Hooper picked at the specks on the lapels of his jacket, then adjusted his necktie, smoothed his hair and focused his gaze on the reflection in the mirror of the woman sprawled provocatively on the bed. Should have been Jess Larson there, he thought, not that two-bit bar girl. Should have been and, damn it, would be once he got to rounding her up, *when* he got to rounding her up, *if* he did.

Where in hell was she, still in town, holed up, somebody hiding her? When he found the sonofabitch who had taken her ...

185

Who was he kidding? It was not Jess Larson who was getting to him, it was the fellow who had slit Zac's throat, who had slipped into that barber's shop soft and silent as a shadow, who had been in town all along, maybe for hours, who was still here.

Quinton!

Hooper grunted and swept a hand over the lapel. Damn dust, clung to a fellow like ... like Frank Quinton! And just when you thought you had brushed him aside, there he was again, only more so. Well, maybe this time the fellow had overplayed his hand. Could only be a matter of time now before the boys dug him out. Couple of hours and they would have the town apart, door by door, window by window, plank by plank if it came to it. Quinton might be a soft mover, but sheer numbers would corner him.

Trouble was, his being here, unseen, unheard, had spooked the town, set the nerves jangling, 'specially with Rand disappearing and now Doc Raynes. Hell, the whole town was picking at dust!

Hooper grunted again, turned from the mirror and crossed to the window. Evening was creeping in; time to move; get some planning into things. Somebody had to keep an edge, just like he had settling the score with Luce Whitworth. Putting him behind bars—and in his own jail at that—had been a real touch of class, all the lying sonofabitch had coming to him. He could hardly wait to see the look on Whitworth's face when it came to the hanging.

The hanging ... He frowned. That would have to come soon, tonight, before folk spooked themselves into stupor. Chances were that once Quinton saw what the town had in mind for Whitworth he would call off the stalking and ride out. Then they could all get back to normal, whatever that was.

Meantime, there were things to be done, organized. Drinks on the house for the boys, that should help. And girls for them who had a mind.

'Yuh leavin' me, Mister Hooper?' cooed the girl from the bed.

'Yuh just stay where yuh are, honey,' grinned Hooper, heading for the door. 'I got a feelin' we're all goin' to be busy tonight.'

'Should've known that washin' would be a waste of time.' Jess Larson shifted to a drier patch of mouldy straw in the abandoned hog-pen and stared hard at Quinton through the gathering night gloom. 'Of all the places yuh could've found ...' She wiped the caked mud and dung from her hands and sniffed loudly. 'Did it have to be here?'

'Last place anybody'd think of lookin',' said Quinton from the other side of the pen. 'Spotted the place on my way to find the doc. Homestead's empty, mile outa town, too far for them huntin' parties of Hooper's to come scratchin'. We're safe enough. And there ain't no hogs!'

'Some deal,' said Jess, raising her eyes to the darkening sky. 'And what now? We stayin' the night, or ...' She paused. 'Not that I ain't grateful to yuh for gettin' me outa town. I am. Things were shapin' up a mite ugly back there. Hooper's rulin' the roost. Whitworth's in jail—'

'I seen,' murmured Quinton.

'Yuh goin' back, aren't yuh? Yuh ain't through, not yet. No, yuh dumb-headed enough to go ridin' into that town for no good reason now than your pride. Can't yuh leave it, Quinton, call it a day? Ain't yuh had your fill?'

'I'll finish when I finish, ma'am, and that's the way of it.'

'Suit y'self,' shrugged the woman. 'But what about Rand and the doc? Yuh can't let them—'

'That's where you come in,' said Quinton. 'Yuh ride out to the trail, go find Doc Raynes, tell him the way of things, let him decide. He'll know what to do.'

'And then?'

'Always took yuh for a resourceful woman, ma'am,' smiled Quinton. 'I guess you'll figure somethin'.'

At about that same time, Willard Hooper was leaning on the bar of the saloon, his keen eyes watching the drinkers, the girls, the players at the two card tables, and wondering just how long he had before the liquor lost its punch, the girls their appeal and the cards their edge.

Not long, he reckoned. The search for Jess Larson and Quinton had drawn a blank. Not a sign or sight of them—which meant that Quinton had found himself some hole out of town to go bury himself. But of a deal more concern to Hooper was the fact that the search had revealed Legget Rand to have left town some time back, packed for a long ride, and that Doc Raynes had left in a hurry.

So could it be, he pondered, that Rand had ridden out to find Quinton, that Luce

Whitworth had mistaken his target and shot Rand but not killed him, and that Quinton had coerced Doc Raynes into tending a wounded man out there on the trail?

He reckoned so—and that left him with the problem of Rand should Doc pull him through. 'Damn!' he hissed through a cloud of cigar smoke. He glanced at the clock above the bar—coming up for ten—then at the night beyond the batwings. Timing, it was all a question of timing. Get it wrong and this whole plan would blow up in his face. Get it right and he would be living in stylish comfort for the rest of his days—with Jess Larson right alongside him, once he had tamed her. Maybe he would make her his partner. She would be a real asset here in the bar. Other places too.

'Yuh standin' on dynamite, Mister Hooper,' murmured the same lean man who had sparked the hanging talk earlier. He leaned closer to Hooper at the bar and fingered an empty glass through a pool of spilled beer. 'T'ain't goin' to take much for this lot to go one way or the other—with yuh or agin yuh. Wouldn't wait too long to find out if I were you.'

Hooper gave the man a quick, dark glance. 'How long?' he croaked.

'An hour. No more. Right now they're easin' up after that search, but no amount of liquor is goin' to hold down feelin' spooked. All they're wonderin' now is when is Quinton comin', and where will he be? They know he ain't dead, that's for sure, not after what happened at the barber's place, and they're figurin' Whitworth lied to them.' The man pushed the glass away. 'Looks like yuh got the whole deck in yuh hands, Mister Hooper. Time yuh got to playin', wouldn't yuh say?'

Hooper brushed cigar ash from his jacket. That was the trouble with most of the good things in life, he thought, they always got so messy. And somebody always had to go clean up.

TWENTY

The boy scrambled on all-fours through a patch of moonlight deep into the darkness of the scrub and brush. His eyes gleamed round and bright as he scanned the tangled maze of twigs, dead wood, roots and rocks. That fool pup sure had a way with him, he thought, wiping a dirt-grubby hand over his face then fixing the set of his floppy hat. Never needed more than half a chance to slip away and this time he had made a real meal of it.

'Packet!' he called softly. 'Hey, Packet, will yuh just get here.'

The boy waited, licking his lips, blinking, listening for the faintest rustle, the telltale rush of panting. Nothing. Darn the dog, just never seemed to get the hang of staying close. One of these days he would push it too far, find himself square-on to some snap-happy coyote out for supper.

'Packet!' called the boy again, and scrambled on.

Maybe it would be better to wait, let the dog come to him. Heck, no, not in the case of Packet. Crazy pup just figured the whole world was his for the nosing out. Could be he would get tired or thirsty, hole-up in some crevice someplace, or head for home if he had the sense. Pa reckoned a dog could find home from almost anywhere. But this was Packet, no ordinary dog by half.

'Packet!'

The boy paused again, flat on his stomach, the smell of the dirt and brush tingling at his nostrils. One thing he had going for him, though, he thought, spitting sand, nobody was going to miss him for a while, not with the town in the state it was. Pa was over at Hooper's—been there most of the day—and Ma was alongside the other women at the church where

Preacher John was saying prayers like a whole year of Sundays had come at once. Just about everybody in town was tied down somewhere. And, heck, they had even clapped Sheriff Whitworth in his own jail!

All to do with that fellow Quinton they said was coming back. Pa reckoned there would be some real wild shooting, and Ma was jumpy like she always was when anybody mentioned trouble. Could be things would get as bad as they did that night way back. That had been real spooky, and Ma had never said a word to Pa for weeks, 'specially after the marshal took that fellow Quinton back to Salton. Ma had figured that all wrong and said as much, just the once so Pa was not mistaking how she felt. Heck, had Pa been tick-itchy after that!

'Packet!'

The boy raised himself on his elbows at the softest sound of a scuff. There was somebody out there, sure enough, but nothing like a wandering pup. No, this was a rider coming down the trail, real slow too, holding his mount to a steady walk. Too dark to see anything, but he could hear the jangle of tack now, the creak of leather. Another minute and the fellow would be right alongside ...

Heck, just supposing it was Quinton!

The boy blinked rapidly, swallowed with a gulp, and shuddered clean through his body at the sudden yap of the dog, snort of the horse, sound of the rider's voice and swish of loose sand. He came slowly, fearfully to his knees, craned higher to see over the tops of the brush—and stared directly into the man's eyes gleaming like stars through the darkness.

'This your dog, boy?' said the man, as the pup pranced excitedly in the sand.

'Yessir,' croaked the boy. 'Name's Packet.'

'Well, Packet, yuh'd best get back where yuh belong.'

The boy brushed quickly through the

scrub and collected the pup in his arms.

'And you got a name, young fella?' asked the man.

'Sam Huckridge, sir.'

'Out a mite late, ain't yuh, Sam?'

'On account of Packet here, sir. He kinda gets to runnin' free when he can.'

The man grunted. 'Freedom's a fine thing, boy. Don't never take it from him. Just teach him how to use it.'

'Yessir.'

The boy blinked rapidly again, aware now of the size and shape of the man silhouetted against the backdrop of the moonlit sky.

'Time yuh were indoors, Sam,' said the man. 'Yuh folks'll be frettin' on yuh.'

'They ain't home right now, sir,' said the boy still blinking, hugging the pup to him. 'Fact, nobody's home. Town's all ...' He saw the man's eyes narrow like dark folds of cloud.

'All what, boy?'

'All kinda waitin', sir. Over at Hooper's

and some in the church with Preacher John,' spluttered the boy. 'They been there most of the day.'

'And what they waitin' on, Sam? Yuh got any idea?'

Sam Huckridge swallowed deeply and tightened his hug on the pup. 'I figure it might be you, sir, if yuh happen to be a fella name of Quinton.'

The man waited a moment, his fingers tight on the reins. 'That's me, Sam,' he murmured. 'Frank Quinton.'

The boy licked at a sudden creep of sweat across his lips. 'Yuh goin' in, sir?' he asked. 'There's an awful lot of 'em there, and my pa says as how—'

'Yuh promise me somethin', Sam?'

'Yessir.'

'Just get y'self and Packet there indoors fast as yuh can. And yuh stay there, boy, no nosin' out.'

'Nossir—I mean, yessir. I promise.'

Quinton smiled softly. 'Good. So yuh move now. Go on, boy, move.'

'Yessir ... Sure thing, sir. Right now.'

And with that Sam Huckridge ran into the night with the pup clutched tight to his chest.

'Time's come, boys,' announced Willard Hooper to the crowded bar. 'We're all through with waitin'. Ain't servin' no purpose puttin' this off. We got a reckonin' to be settled so we'd best get to it. Yuh all with me?'

There were shouts of support; chairs were pushed back from laden tables; girls dismissed from aching knees; drinks finished in a single gulp; arms stretched; hands rubbed together anxiously.

Hooper straightened his jacket and leaned closer to the man at his side. 'We get to this fast,' he murmured. 'I don't want no messin'. Sooner it's over—'

'What about Quinton?' called a man from the other side of the bar. 'He ain't showed.'

'How do yuh know he ain't?' came a tight retort.

'S'right,' clipped a man at the batwings. 'Could be out there now.'

'Don't matter none,' shouted Hooper. 'If he's here he'll see what we're about soon enough. If he ain't, that's his affair.'

'Hooper's right,' said the lean man, pushing himself clear of the bar. 'Quinton can figure things for himself. This town ain't answerin' to nobody save itself. Benefice does as Benefice reckons!'

'That's more like it!' shouted a man waving a half-empty bottle. 'And to hell with them who says other!'

The batwings were pushed open as the crowd surged and staggered to the street, turning like the flow of a stream for the jail. Voices rose in eager chants and wild calls. Some men stumbled, others grabbed them; one man fell face-down in the dirt and stayed there as the crowd passed over him. A bar girl caught in the tide had her dress ripped clean from her body and ran screaming to the boardwalk. A hitched mount tugged nervously at the rail and snorted madly, finally breaking free and disappearing into the darkness.

Hooper, with the lean man close behind, shouldered his way to the head of the crowd as it reached the jail, stepped to the door and raised an arm for silence.

'Hold it there, boys,' he shouted. 'I'll bring him out. Somebody go fix the noose.' He nodded to the lean man and murmured, 'Keep 'em quiet. I'll do this my way.'

There was only the softest glow of light from the lantern on the turnkey's desk as Willard Hooper closed the door to the jail behind him and peered into the shadows.

'Sam,' he said, straining to see ahead of him. 'Sam—where the devil are yuh? Yuh supposed to be ...'

He heard the grunt before he saw the open cell door and the turnkey trussed and gagged in a corner; saw the frenzied look in the man's gaze, the blood trickling from the gash on the side of his head, and felt his own blood run suddenly cold and thin through his veins.

'What the hell happened here?' he croaked, pulling the gag from the turnkey's mouth. 'Where's Whitworth?'

'He jumped me, Mister Hooper,' spluttered the man. 'Caught me cold with some talk about—'

'Never mind,' snapped Hooper. 'Where's he now? Where'd he go, yuh blunderin' idiot?'

'I don't know, Mister Hooper. I ain't no idea. He just went, a good hour back.'

Hooper wiped the sweat from his face as he turned slowly to stare at the door to the street and hear the baying of the mob beyond it.

TWENTY-ONE

'Shut yuh mouths, all of yuh! Shut 'em!' Willard Hooper stood with his back to the jailhouse wall, the sweat hot and sticky across his spine, lathering his face, trickling between his fingers; his gaze dancing over the stares of the mob in the street like a moth at a flame. 'I ain't takin' no blame for this. Whitworth jumped Sam. Could've happened to any one of yuh.'

'Yeah,' cracked a voice, 'but where's Whitworth now?'

'Yeah,' followed another, 'where's he now?'

Hooper licked anxiously at his lips, glanced quickly at the lean man alongside him. 'Can't have gotten far,' he croaked. 'Can't have, not t'night. Chances are he's still in town. Holed-up some place.' His gaze danced. 'Hell, there aren't that many places a fella can hide.'

'So where do we start?' shouted a man.

'Well ...' spluttered Hooper.

'Start at the livery,' said the lean man, stepping forward. 'Dozen of yuh get over there now. Rest of yuh spread y'selves down the street. Don't miss nothin', understand? And when yuh find him, keep him alive. We ain't got to the real business yet.'

The mob began to murmur and shuffle, talking among themselves, glancing Hooper's way from time to time as if to confirm an opinion. Or was it a decision?

'Yuh heard the man,' shouted Hooper. 'Get to it. We're wastin' time.'

'We been wastin' time most of the day, Mister Hooper,' said a man at the front of the mob. 'Watchin' out for Quinton, then lookin' for that woman. Now Whitworth. We ain't gettin' nowheres.'

'They're soberin' up,' murmured the lean man at Hooper's ear. 'Do somethin'.'

'Sure, boys,' smiled Hooper. 'Feel the

same m'self. Warm work with it, eh?' He mopped at his brow. 'So what say we go have ourselves a drink? Freshen up. What yuh say? And all on me, boys, all on me. Don't need to put a hand to yuh pockets. Yuh with me?'

The mob might have moved then, might have set out for the saloon, keen to get to the drinks and the girls, but not a man among them moved at the eerie, echoing sound of horses, riders heading out of the night towards them like lost ghosts.

The mob fell silent and turned as one man to the sounds. More than one rider and coming on real slow, tired and worn whoever they were.

'That ain't Quinton, that's for sure,' came the call as a half-dozen broke from the mob and went ahead.

'Goddamnit, it's Doc Raynes!'

'Legget Rand with him.'

'And the woman!'

Hooper felt another surge of sweat at his spine, the tingling in the hot lather on his face. 'Hell!' he hissed.

'This just ain't your night, Mister Hooper,' murmured the lean man, through a cynically twisted grin. 'We mebbe goin' to have to think again. Yuh reckon?'

Hooper groaned and strode into the street. 'Let 'em through there?' he bellowed. 'Let 'em through!'

Doc Raynes raised a hand to halt his party and stared at Hooper. 'If yuh wanna know what happened out there on the trail, Rand here'll be happy to tell yuh once he's capable.' The doc's stare was steady, tight as a beam of light on Hooper's face. 'Meantime, me and Jess Larson are goin' to do the best we can for him over at my place. Rand's hit bad, but he'll live.' Doc Raynes paused a moment, turning his gaze on the mob. 'Somebody had best go tell Luce Whitworth—tell him he's got another ghost comin' out to haunt him.'

No one moved, no one spoke as the party moved away into the shadowed gloom of the street.

'So now what, Mister Hooper?' called a man from the crowd. 'We go get Whitworth, or stand here waitin' for Quinton? Which hell we starin' into, f'Crissake?'

Luce Whitworth bundled the three shivering bar girls and the barman into the back room of the saloon, closed and locked the door and leaned back on it through a long, rasping sigh, his eyes closing on the blurred swirl of tables, chairs, the flotsam of drinkers, the low curls of lingering smoke. When he opened them again he blinked on the sting of cold sweat and swallowed over a throat as parched as a bone-dead creek stream.

His fingers fell instinctively to the butt of his holstered Colt, tapped it as if seeking reassurance, hovered, then clenched to a fist. 'Easy, Luce, easy,' he murmured to himself. There was no rush, not yet. Things were going his way, slowly, step by careful step. All he needed to do now was keep his head, think straight, stay calm. And wide awake.

He licked the salty sweat clear of his lips, blinked again and moved to the bar. He needed a drink, long and cool, something to sate a deep thirst. Maybe a beer would do it; maybe two beers. Keep him steady, give him time to think through the next move.

Willard Hooper could go to hell, he thought, gulping on the frothing jar, and he would, damn it, moment he stepped through them batwings. No messing, no talking, nothing. Just lead, plumb in the middle of his rolling gut. And when that was done ... well, one step at a time. Keep it straight, keep it easy. No panic, no rush.

But there was still Quinton.

He could feel the fellow in his bones. Must have made a mistake out there on the trail, shot some other sonofabitch. Maybe Rand. So what? Who needed Legget Rand? Not Benefice. Should have finished him that night of the lynching, anyhow. 'Yeah, the hangin',' he murmured. Maybe he should get to hanging Willard Hooper. Hang him high like the two-bit hound he was.

But there was still Quinton.

Where the hell was Quinton? Had to be here some place. Right here in town, or still waiting a mile or so outside, lurking in the night like some scheming rattler? Or would he make his move come sun-up? That would be more his style; light at his back, stare cold as stone. So let him. Town would be a different place at first light. Hooper, for one, would be dead and all Quinton would see and hear when he rode in would be the undertaker making up a coffin. Get himself a good look at a premonition.

Whitworth smiled to himself and finished his beer. Meantime, what was keeping Hooper?

He could hear the hum of the mob far end of the street, hear the raised shouts, the sudden silences and imagine the look on the sweating faces at the news that the jail cell was empty and Luce Whitworth on the loose again. Should give Hooper and that lean, mean sidekick of his something to chew over. But how would the mob figure things now: go on the rampage in search of a neck, any neck, to stretch; turn on Hooper; wait for Quinton? One thing they would not be doing yet awhile was heading for their beds. Chances were, in fact, that they would be back for more liquor. Any minute now.

Whitworth moved quickly to a window. Not a deal to be seen from there, he decided, then crossed the bar again to the stairway to the upper rooms. That was the place to be, he reckoned, up there on the shadowed balcony with a clear view of the whole of the saloon. Pick off a target at will from there; take Hooper, and maybe Quinton, whenever he chose.

He smiled softly to himself as he bounded up the stairs and slid silently into the shadows, missing in his haste the gleam of the two eyes watching him from the deeper darkness.

Liquor them up some, get them back in the palm of his hand, pass the girls around, have themselves a real night of it, then strike when the going was at its best. That was the way, thought Hooper, walking ahead of the mob to the saloon. He had used the strategy before; he could use it again the minute they got their hands on Whitworth. There would be a hanging this night, so help him there would. Somebody's neck would be in the noose, and maybe more than one if they got to finding Quinton. Hell, he thought, that sonofabitch was ... just that, a sonofa-goddamn-bitch!

Hooper was within a step of the batwings and about to reach for them, when he stopped, the sweat suddenly cold on his face, his nerve-ends tingling as if dipped into ice. Place was too quiet, he thought, too empty. Where was the barman, the girls? If any of them had thought they were taking the rest of the night off ...

And then he heard the creaking, the slow, strained creak of a rope taut and twisting under the drag of a heavy weight. The sort of noise he had heard before, long back, on that night all those years ago when they had left the body of Ben Little turning dead-eyed on the hanging tree.

TWENTY-TWO

The body of Luce Whitworth was hanging from a rope dropped into the space of the saloon from the first-floor balcony. He was hatless, stripped of his sidearm and boots, and the sweat on his face, mixed with the saliva from his lolling mouth, was still wet. He had been hanged, someone said, only minutes ago.

Hooper crossed the saloon with slow, measured steps, his gaze fixed, as if hypnotized, on the turning body, his arms loose at his sides, the lean sidekick two steps behind him, the mob hovering like a smothering of quiet flies at the batwings. There were no sounds save for the creak of the rope, the fall of steps, and then nothing when Hooper finally stood beneath the body and stared into the bulbous thrust of its eyes.

'Quinton!' he hissed, and in the next moment had spun round to the mob. 'Quinton's doin',' he croaked. 'He's here, goddamn him! Right here!' He spun again to rake his gaze wildly over the balcony. 'Quinton!' be bellowed. 'Quinton, damn yuh, show y'self. Let me see yuh, f'Crissake!'

The rope creaked as if caught in the blast of Hooper's breath. Someone in the mob shifted a foot. The lean sidekick's fingers spread to the butt of his Colt.

'Yuh comin' down, Quinton?' roared Hooper. 'Yuh got the guts, or yuh just goin' to hide there?' The sweat broke clear and glistening on his face. 'Well, yuh ain't got no place to go, not now yuh ain't. Yuh trapped, Quinton, yuh hear that? There's more guns here—'

But that was as far as Hooper got as a sudden salvo of shots ripped into the floorboards at his feet sending him skidding against a loaded table, scattering glasses and bottles. Another blaze blasted a window to flying shards, a third skimmed across the bar like a lick of raging flame. The mob backed to the boardwalk. A girl screamed from behind the locked back-room door. Hooper dropped to his knees in the cover of the upturned table and gazed wide-eyed at the sidekick.

'Do somethin', will yuh?' he rasped. 'Get the sonofabitch!'

The lean man dived for the stairway, Colt drawn and firm in his hand, and had mounted a half-dozen steps when the roar from a gun above him tossed him back as if caught in the whirl of a tornado, spreadeagled him across the floor and left him bloodsoaked and staring empty-eyed into Hooper's face.

Hooper shuddered and twisted round to face the mob. 'Where are yuh all?' he yelled. 'Can't yuh see we got Quinton cold up there? He can't go no place. He's finished. Just get y'selves in here, all of yuh, damn yuh! Let's end it, put that sonofabitch out of his misery. Take him alive, if yuh like. We'll go hang him like we said. Who's for that? Who's for a hangin'?'

No one moved, no one spoke. All eyes were tight on the balcony, every breath heavy as rock in every chest as the mob waited, chained like lost souls to where they stood.

'Yellow-bellied scum!' roared Hooper, clambering to his feet, swaying as he struggled to draw his Colt. 'Not a man among yuh! Never was. You're all vermin, yuh hear me? Vermin! Scum and vermin! Well, I'll show yuh. I'll show yuh who's runnin' this goddamn town now. And when I'm through, I'll hang every one of yuh! Every last one! Here, in this bar—just like the bastard danglin' there!'

Hooper fired two fast shots into the hanged man, spinning the body round until its creaking, groaning momentum broke the rope clear of its hold and dropped the lifeless Luce Whitworth to the floor with a sickening thud.

'Now for Quinton!' bellowed Hooper, and charged for the stairs in a lather of flying sweat and swinging limbs. He reached the third step, tripped, crawled forward and was on his feet again when the shadow spread like a long, dark stain ahead of him.

Hooper froze where he stood, his gun arm loose at his side, his mouth open, eyes wet with sweat and the sudden stinging ache of fear, as Quinton watched him from the balcony.

'Yuh goin'to use that thing, Hooper, or are your hands fit for only noosin' a fella? Suggest yuh make yuh mind up fast. It's gettin' late.'

Hooper's lips twitched through words that were never formed, never left his mouth. He waited, staring, sweating, the breath rattling in his throat, then raised the gun as if lifting a weight from a great depth.

'Your choice, mister,' murmured Quinton, 'but it's quicker this way. Messy, but quicker.'

And when Quinton's Colt roared, the night and the town of Benefice blazed with a light that screamed *Go to Hell!*

Legget Rand opened one eye on the bright, sunlit afternoon, sighed, and settled again in the chair on the shadowed veranda at Doc Raynes's back door. Too warm to move, he decided, and a darned sight too early. Fellow recovering from a gunshot wound needed time and quiet; no need to stir much before sundown. No cause either, come to that.

He sighed again. On the other hand there was a deal to be done around town: saloon cleaned up, livery and barber's shop reopened, that darned hanging tree cut down—and it was time somebody got to appointing a new sheriff. Town without law was a town without order. Luce Whitworth had proved that plain enough.

He grunted. Would have given a deal, he thought, to have seen Quinton settling the scores, not that there was any shortage of tongues ready to tell it again and again. Must have been quite a night ... Quinton's night, for sure. Maybe he would get to hearing from the fellow himself when he was good and ready, and before he left town as talk had it he would. Well, maybe ... And then there was Jess Larson. What in hell was to become of her?

'Yuh got a visitor,' said Doc Raynes, stepping from the back room to Rand's side. 'Marshal Edgeworth.'

Rand's eyes stayed closed. 'That so,' he murmured. 'What's he here for this time?'

'Payin' my respects,' smiled Edgeworth, taking a chair facing Rand. 'Only ever seem to see yuh when you're recoverin' from a gunfight.'

'That weren't no gunfight, Marshal. That was that sonofabitch Whitworth mistakin' me for Quinton. But I ain't complainin'.

I survived—and Quinton got his justice.' Rand opened one eye. 'That's the way of it, ain't it? That why yuh here?'

'Pickins rode out from Kneebone. Told me the way of things, and now I've seen Quinton himself and heard how it was. He's in the clear, a free man. Ain't got nothin' on him, save the shame of my mistake. I was wrong, Legget, right down the line. And took five years out of a man's life. Hell!'

'Well, I'm sure as hell glad to hear yuh say that,' said Rand, opening both eyes. 'Yuh should've listened ... Never mind. It's done now. We can do without the likes of Hooper and Whitworth—and I just hope this town has learned a lesson. Came as close as it'll ever come to runnin' into a hell of its own makin'.'

Edgeworth relaxed. 'Don't want to see or hear the likes of it again,' he said thoughtfully. 'And I won't, not with the law-keeping back in your hands.'

'Me?' croaked Rand, struggling upright

in the chair. 'Part-lame old has-been like me! Hell, Marshal, yuh sure scratchin' at worn stone if yuh figure—'

'Worn mebbe,' said Edgeworth, 'but that don't include the thinkin'. Whitworth put yuh out that night of the lynchin'. Townsfolk know that, and now they want yuh back, right where yuh belonged all along.' He leaned forward. 'What yuh say, Legget? Yuh'll take the badge? Doc here reckons yuh'll be up to it.'

'Does he now?' grunted Rand, leaning back, closing his eyes again. 'Well, we'll see—come sundown.'

And then he smiled.

Frank Quinton finished the saddling up, patted the mount's neck and led it quietly from the livery into the blaze of afternoon sunlight. Should make good miles before nightfall, he reckoned, maybe clear the hill range, heading due West. And glad of it too, he thought. Glad to shake the dust of Benefice from him, put this whole miserable episode into the past—and get to making up on five lost years. That should make for interesting times, beginning with—

He turned at the sudden swish of skirts behind him and stared wide-eyed at the sight of Jess Larson. And just what, he wondered, was this—sky-blue dress, lace-trimmed, hair tied back to a matching bow, and a look on the woman's face he had never thought might be there.

'Well,' she asked, completing a pirouette, 'what yuh think? Yuh like it?' Her eyes flashed. 'Brand new. Fresh from the store this mornin'.'

'That sure is somethin', ma'am,' murmured Quinton. 'Never thought—'

'As yuh'd see the day?' she smiled. 'Well, now yuh have. And this time I ain't plannin' on spendin' a night in no hog-pen!'

'So where are yuh spendin' it?'

'That depends, Mister Quinton. I might get to havin' m'self one of them real classy dinners, with wine and candles and that, or I might ... Well, I guess it depends on who I'm spendin' it with.' The smile faded. 'Don't look to be y'self, not from the way yuh got that horse packed.'

' 'Fraid not, ma'am. Pullin' out soon as I can. Want to clear the hills before dark.' Quinton turned back to the mount. 'Yuh stayin' on here?' he asked.

'Depends,' said Jess softly.

'Awful lot of dependin' goin' on.'

'And so there is too. Heck, Quinton, yuh can't just ride out like that, not after all that's happened. Why do yuh think I stayed with yuh like I did? Weren't curiosity, that's for sure.'

'So why did yuh?' asked Quinton.

Jess Larson settled her hands tight on her hips. 'Well, mebbe it's 'cus I wanted to make sure yuh got y'self a decent pair of boots!' The smile glowed on her face again. 'Catch yuh up in an hour, soon as I've changed and packed.'

'And bring the dress with yuh,' grunted

Quinton. 'Mebbe we'll find some place for yuh to wear it!'

Quinton was a half-mile out of Benefice when he reined up alongside Sam Huckridge and his pup. 'That dog still runnin' free, boy?' he asked.

'Nossir, walkin' right at my heels. Kinda got the hang of it, I guess,' grinned Sam.

'Keep it that way,' said Quinton, and rode on.

'Hey, Mister Quinton,' called the boy, 'I saw what happened back there. Saw yuh take Hooper. That was some shootin', eh? Ain't never seen shootin' like that. Yuh comin' back, Mister Quinton? Yuh ain't leavin', are yuh?'

But the rider was already no more than a blur of grey dust.